T0149431

The Turtle Woman

A Fantastic Romance

Esther Murbach

authorHOUSE®

AuthorHouse™
1663 Liberty Drive
Bloomington, IN 47403
www.authorhouse.com
Phone: 1-800-839-8640

First published by AuthorHouse   01/06/2012

ISBN: 978-1-4678-8184-5 (sc)
ISBN: 978-1-4678-8185-2 (ebk)

Printed in the United States of America

Contents

Acknowledgements

First of all, my thanks for inspiration and help go to the Irish tour director who prefers to remain anonymous. His verdict of "It's good!" after reading the first twenty-three pages of the manuscript gave me the motivation to go on.

I am indebted to my neighbour and friend Mariana Streiff, who was with me through every stage of the writing process and gave me valuable constructive criticism.
Thank you, Mariana!

Preface

I began writing my fourth book in spring 2011, starting with some of my childhood memories. I wrote it in my native German tongue. It was supposed to become a mix of memoirs and fiction, but somehow the spark was missing. Summer came, and my friend Edith suggested we take a holiday together, preferably a tour around Ireland. So we did. We set out on a big coach from Dublin going south, then clockwise up to the northwest and down again on the east. After Dublin our first stop was Glendalough, and there it happened. I started falling in love with Ireland. The love grew with every day and every stage of the tour, until I was totally hooked on the Emerald Isle. Some of my enthusiasm, and not only mine, was due to the competence and inner fire of our guide, a real Irish patriot. It was my first encounter with one of the most incredible species in the world, a race of full-blooded multi-taskers bred by the Irish Tourist Board—the Irish tour director.

An Irish tour director is a true phenomenon. He consists of at least a dozen specialists rolled into one, namely driver, porter, guide, historian, lecturer, route planner, psychologist, nurse, social worker, trouble-shooter, disc jockey, entertainer, and sometimes live singer. He must have kissed the Blarney Stone, which bestows the gift of eloquence on the kisser, at least ten times. Keeping up a positive mood and memorizing a load of the worst mother-in-law-jokes is compulsory. And most important of all, he must know all the shamrock gift shops with attached toilets in the whole country and must lead his flock to them at well-calculated intervals. Afterwards, said flock has to be shooed back into the coach on time and without the help of a border collie. A head count three times over is recommended. The only thing not expected from the tour director is carrying pampers on the coach. An occasional pampering of difficult customers may at times be required though.

To make a long story short, the trip did its trick. The spark was ignited. Back in Switzerland I adapted what I had written so far into English and changed the concept of the narrative. A big part of the plot was moved to Ireland, which forced me (forced?) to go back again two months later for research. After all, I needed a further look at the country of my inspiration. I set up base in Galway for two weeks, where on the day after my arrival whom should I bump into by pure coincidence? None other than the tour director from the summer tour. We sat together, and I gently broke the news to him that I planned to use him partly as a role model for the hero of this tale. He graciously bent to the inevitable and agreed to supervise my text, correcting any errors about Ireland I might commit.

The tale speaks in a symbolic way of what Ireland and its incredible spiritual energy can do to some people. It awakens you, changes you, and turns your world upside down. If it does that, you'll never recover from the experience. The Irish smile in your heart will stay forever until the end of your days.

Esther Murbach, 2011

The Country Child

When I was small, I lived in the country with my grandparents. I never asked myself why I lived with my grandparents. All the other children in the village lived with their parents, but I didn't miss having parents. I belonged to GrannyPa, and they belonged to me. I called them GrannyPa because to me they were a unity, a symbiosis, though at the time I didn't know the word "symbiosis" and what it meant. Of course I knew GrannyPa were really two people, but it took me some years to realize they did not always feel and think as one. As long as I saw them as one, belonging to me and loving me as one, my world was perfect.

My world, our world, was the little village of Idylliken in the green hills of the upper Baselbiet, a rural area about thirty kilometres from the city of Basel. The river Ergolz flowed placidly through the meadows in a shallow curve not far from the old farmhouse where we lived. There was a small sandbank in the curve, with many pebbles and other interesting objects washed up by the clear rippling waters. Often I would say to GrannyPa that I was going to collect "precious stones" on the sandbank, and every time I would get the same reply, uttered with a mix of concern and tolerant understanding of a child's need to do things on her own: "Don't fall into the water!" Never would they have tried to keep me from my forays, whether to the riverbank or to the forest or to the neighbour's stable. When I brought back coloured stones or polished glass shards from the riverbank, which to me were jewels, they would admire them with me and let me put them in a little wooden box, padded inside with one of Granny's embroidered hankies, and hide them in the cupboard so that no thief would find them.

When I grew older and started reading—long before I was due to go to school—I learnt things that took away some of my childish beliefs and illusions. It began with me identifying the letters in the book of fairy tales GrannyPa used to read to me over and over again. I watched their fingers follow the lines, asking more and more questions instead of just listening. "What is this sign? What does that one mean?" Patiently they explained the letters to me, the sounds they stood for, how they were assembled to form words and meanings. One day I took the book out of GrannyPa's hands. "I can tell the story myself now," I said. "You listen." So the bedtime story routine was turned around. I read to GrannyPa—to either of them or both of them—haltingly at first but soon fluently, savouring every word that took on a meaning in front of my eyes.

"She is so precocious," Grandpa used to say proudly to the man in the shop across the road where he took me to buy cologne. He needed the cologne for his barbershop, where all the farmers from the village came to get a shave or a haircut. Invariably he slapped the pungently smelling liquid on their cheeks after every shave, no matter how much it burnt a freshly scraped skin. His customers took it stoically. No one complained.

He was the expert, and he knew what was best. If Carl made your skin burn, it must be for a good reason.

Carl. That was his name. To me, he was just Grandpa whom I loved unconditionally and who loved me. He never slapped me with cologne, never burnt my skin. Carl the barber was a different person, albeit an interesting one. I liked to watch and listen while he served his clients. He whipped up froth from a white powder mixed with water in a china bowl, smeared it on their ruddy cheeks with a round brush, and then scraped it off with a shiny perfectly honed knife. He honed the knives himself. The handle of the brush came from the horn of an unlucky cow; the bristles were the unwilling donation of a badger. He would slide the froth mixed with the cut-off stubbles from the knife back into the bowl. I thought the formerly pristine white matter looked especially ugly when the stubbles in it were black. A swipe or two with a wet towel removed the rest of the foam from the client's face, and then came the cologne.

In the shop across the road I had to stand on my toes to raise my nose over the high wooden counter, where the shopkeeper put the cologne after taking it from a shelf. Self-service had not yet reached the little village store. I didn't know what "precocious" meant, but I heard the pride in Grandpa's voice, so it must be something good.

Many years later I saw it in a different light. Being precocious also meant that the pain was worse when you understood about grown-up things but were still a child without grown-up

3

defences. Reading put an end to my innocence. My compulsive devouring of printed matter included anything I could lay my eyes on—Granny's cooking recipes, dusty books I found in the attic, magazines in Grandpa's barber shop, tattered by the rough fingers of impatient customers while waiting for their turn under the knife or scissors. It was in one of these magazines that I first saw a picture of Siamese twins and the caption to go with it. It said that they lived in a "symbiosis" and that they were tied to each other for life, for better and for worse, without any alternative, whether they got on with each other or not—and often they did not. They were two minds in one duplex body, longing to be disengaged. Secretly I cried, but I couldn't talk about it to GrannyPa, for they didn't like me to read all those magazines, even though they were not able to keep me away from them all the time. So I was on my own, trying to process the twins' tragedy in my precocious mind. Also, there was this word in the caption which I didn't fully understand and which frightened me. "Freaks", it said. The twins considered themselves as "freaks". It sounded terrible. I hated the word at first sight. Many years later I remembered it as a premonition of what was happening to me, the freak I was turning into myself.

However, my first six years were painless and magic. Magic filled the old farmhouse we lived in, barely heatable in winter but full of interesting nooks and crannies. Sometimes I saw shiny little spectres sitting in the dark corners, for instance on the circular staircase which wound up to the first floor. They were friendly spectres, smiling and waving to me with tiny transparent hands. One of them would always put a finger to his mouth, as if I didn't know that this was a secret between them and me, that I could see them and nobody else could. They acted as my glow worms when I had to go upstairs and the light from the dim naked bulb hanging from the ceiling had failed again, or if I peeped into other dark places of the old building, like the empty stables where GrannyPa once had kept a cow and two goats. The animals were long gone, but sometimes I could see their shapes against the black wooden walls, hardly visible and glassy like soap bubbles. Slowly the bubbly cow would turn her head to look at me with friendly complacent eyes. So did the goats, moving somewhat faster than the cow. It never occurred to me to stroke them; I knew my touch would make them burst. Of course they were a secret too, for my eyes only.

Never was I afraid in that old house. And for all its lack of comfort, I never felt uncomfortable, but always comforted within its walls—as long as I was little. I didn't know then how lucky I was.

Attached to the house was a large shed with one door on the east side and one on the south side, both leading onto the grassland. The doors were made of rough planks with large slits between them. They were vertical boards stabilized by two horizontal ones, one on top, one on the bottom, and a diagonal one connecting the two. All the boards were fixed together merely with iron nails gone rusty with time and weather. From time to time Grandpa got his tools and hammered a new nail into the wood next to an old rotting one. Usually the doors were open all day long, closed at night, but hardly ever locked. In the big rusty locks the equally rusty keys could barely be turned. They were left in the locks anyway, even if GrannyPa did lock up on some nights. Any amateur thief would have laughed his head off at this, but there were apparently no thieves in our village. Or if there were, those doors signalled to them clearly that there was nothing worth stealing.

Next to the south door was the outhouse, located inside the shed, a wooden cabin with a heart-shaped hole on the upper side of the door. The door could be locked only from the inside with an iron hook. Needless to say, it was rusty like the nails but still functional. The outhouse didn't smell good. But what could you expect from a wooden bench with an open round hole in the middle, where the contents of your insides drop directly into a pit? Once a year a man came with a big cart holding a big barrel and pumped everything up. He collected all the manure in the village and then spread it on the fields, even on GrannyPa's grassland and orchards. So we gave back to the land what we had taken from it, from the grass and the fruit trees and the vegetable patches and the corn fields. For a few days the stench was everywhere, and I was not allowed to walk on the grass until the next rain washed the waste into the ground. Nobody was concerned about hygiene and disease and contamination. Things had been handled like this for centuries in a world where chemical fertilizers and water closets had not yet taken over. But now chemicals and bathrooms had advanced to every small village in the province, and only a few strongholds of the old ways remained, like the house of GrannyPa.

Many years before I was born, sewers were introduced to the village so that every house might profit from modern sanitation. However, Grandpa was not willing to pay for "unnecessary stuff". He refused to give his consent to the envoys of the Idylliken council to have the house connected to the "modern gimmicks" in the trenches. The hole in the bench had served him and his ancestors well enough since the house had been built in the middle of the eighteenth century. Granny had no say in the matter; the decision was naturally up to the patriarch. For some reason the subject of the sewers came up again many years later, and I overheard GrannyPa discussing it. For the first time I noticed a disagreement between the Siamese twins who were my Grandparents. Granny's lips went thin and her whole face sour; Grandpa got loud.

Secretly I sided with Granny in the question of sewers. I was sometimes allowed to use the water closet in the attic of the baker's house across the road. Fascinated, I would watch the water and what I had dropped in it swirl away and disappear down the drain with a gurgling sound. Sometimes I couldn't resist pulling the handle, which swung from a chain attached to the water reservoir on top, a second and a third time. When scolded by the baker's daughter that this was a waste of water, I pretended the toilet paper hadn't gone down the first time or even the second.

The baker's daughter was called Margrit. She was my age and she had a swing in the attic next to the toilet. I was allowed to use the swing as well, and sometimes the baker's wife gave us cookies fresh from the oven in the bake house. That was when bakers still made many things themselves—the breads, the rolls, the cakes, the cookies, the biscuits, and even the ice cream. I loved the baker's house and shop because it always smelt so good, of freshly baked bread and vanilla. I'll never forget that vanilla smell. To this day I love a whiff of vanilla, wherever, whenever. I especially liked the vanilla ice the baker scraped from a freezer at the back of the shop, pressing the yellow scoops into a biscuit cone, which of course came from his bake house too. I paid for the ice with the coins Grandpa sometimes slipped into my hand. He might be stingy when it came to sewerage, but he sure was generous when I was in need of an ice cream.

Once I spent the ice-cream money on a roll of toilet paper. I got it from the shop next to the baker's, the same shop where Grandpa got his cologne. Grandpa had sent me to the shop all by myself. It made me very proud that he trusted me with the purchase of the cologne. On an impulse, I asked the shopkeeper for toilet paper, for one of the rolls I saw sitting on a shelf. He counted my ice-cream money, saying, "It's not enough, but never mind; give me the rest next time." I came home proudly with the soft white paper and placed it on the dining table next to the bottle of cologne. That was the first time I saw Grandpa really angry with me. It didn't last long, but it was a frightening experience.

"I gave you the money for ice cream. Who told you to waste it on unnecessary stuff? There's enough paper in the house. Luxury is for the rich people in the city!"

I started crying, and Granny gave him a look I had never seen on her before. He calmed down at once.

"It's all right," he said gruffly. "Just this once, but don't do it again without asking."

Then he put me on his lap, wiped the tears from my cheeks with a grubby hanky, and kissed me on the forehead. He even gave me new ice-cream money with the explicit order not to spend it on anything else. I nodded and ran to the baker's.

The white paper roll didn't last long. When it came to an end, Granny and I resorted to our old habits of cutting up old newspapers and phone books. We cut the sheets of paper into squares, made small heaps of them, stabbed a hole in a corner of each heap with the thinner blade of the scissors, pulled a piece of string through the hole with the help of a crochet hook, and knotted the ends of the string together. Granny's bundles were very neat, mine a little less so, but I was getting better with practice. The bundles were placed on the bench of the outhouse next to the round opening. I didn't like those bundles and what the paper did to my you-know-what. The newspaper leaves were slightly absorbent, but they left smears of black ink on my skin, which in turn left traces on my underpants. The phone book paper was of a glassy consistency, not absorbent at all. It didn't leave black smears, but it had hardly any cleansing effect at all.

We didn't have hot water in the kitchen. There was a tap with only cold water. The water had to be heated on the wood fire burning in the hearth where GrannyPa cooked their meals. Granny also boiled our underwear and other white textiles in a big pot on the hearth. It was hard work doing the laundry by hand—all the stiff white sheets, the underwear, the towels, and the shirts Grandpa wore day and night. One shirt had to do for a whole week; on Sunday mornings he would change into a fresh one. Granny always managed to get the white cottons and linens really white and spotless, boiling and then scrubbing them on the washboard, rinsing them many times, and using old recipes on stubborn stains. I didn't wonder at the time how she did it, only many years later when I was grown up and when there was a washing machine in every household.

At least I could help Granny a little with hanging up the laundry, lifting the pieces from the wicker basket and handing them to her to put them on the washing line in the garden, and fixing them with ancient wooden pegs.

Years later GrannyPa would buy an electric cooking stove and give the laundry out to a neighbour who had a washing machine. That was after my time with them, and Granny would never be happy with the results of the machine washing. But she had become too weak for hard physical work, so she had to be content with administering some aftercare to the textiles, still using her old tinctures on tenacious stains the machine had not been able to take away.

For washing the dishes, the water also had to be heated on the hearth and poured into the sink. Soap flakes were added, and the dishes were scrubbed with a straggly brush and rinsed with cold water from the tap. Sometimes I did the wiping with a linen cloth. Most of Granny's linen cloths wore ornamental edgings she had embroidered herself. Granny was great at embroidering, at crocheting, sewing and knitting, too.

Actually, she was a school teacher who taught all those things to the village girls twice a week in the little village school not far from our house. A tiny bell in a tiny tower on the roof of the school called the hours, and woe to the girls who were not sitting at their desks when the last sound of the bell died away! Granny was a stern teacher. Sometimes I was allowed to go to the school and sneak into the classroom just before the lesson ended. The big girls would make a fuss of me. "Emily, come sit with me! No, with me, with me!" In the classroom Granny showed a manner much different from the gentle quietness with which she treated me. Then she reminded me of Carl the barber, when he wasn't being my Grandpa but proudly executing his powers over subdued customers who didn't dare to contradict him when he elaborated his views about God and the World, while his scissors clattered over their scalps like bad-tempered storks, or his sharp knives executed slow pirouettes on their faces, or when he finally handed out the cologne torture.

Granny's first name was Frieda, but the girls had to address her as "mistress", which sounded funny to me. All austere authority in her function as a teacher, Granny called the girls to order, to be quiet and bend to their task until the bell tolled. When that happened, they had to put their handiwork away in cotton satchels they had sewn themselves. Each satchel had stitched the name of the girl it belonged to on it. Only after the satchels were locked up in a cupboard did Granny dismiss the girls. They hugged and kissed me and asked me to come again—"Will you, Emily? And next time you'll sit with me!" Finally, Granny shooed them out of the room, took my hand, and allowed me to walk her home.

At home I got private classes in handiwork from Granny. I didn't mind them and was proud of the first button I could sew on myself. But as to manual creation, I preferred the drawing of pictures. With the coloured pencils Granny had bought me, I mostly drew animals and flowers on every piece of paper I could get hold of. That was my second passion after reading.

My thoughts are leading me astray; let's get back to the dishwashing. Machines which did that for you were not in every household yet, and certainly not in GrannyPa's. When GrannyPa worked at the ancient stone sink, they had to bend low, for the sink had been designed 200 years ago for shorter people. The sink was placed under the small kitchen window, which had a view onto Granny's cottage garden on the west side of the house. On the bottom of the sink a hole lead directly through the wall to the outside. Stuck in the hole was a precisely fitted wooden plug. After washing our hands, our teeth, or the dishes, the plug was taken out so that the dirty water would flow out of the house, down along the wall, and into the ground. It left a brownish-grey trail on the wall and a mouldy smell in the air. The lack of sewers left its traces.

Next to the strip of ground drenched with waste water, a narrow lane plastered with stone slabs led around GrannyPa's little garden. There was a flowery part and a vegetable part; the latter was the bigger one. Granny kept lettuce, potatoes, carrots, beans, green peas, and various kinds of berries in the garden. For most berries we had to do nothing but pluck them from the bushes when they were ripe. But the strawberries were a problem, and the lettuce too. We were at war with the snails. Every day we gathered snails away from their favourite meals and drowned them in a bowl filled with beer. In most of the other plants the snails had no interest, but they were not the only threat to our crop. As to the potatoes, it was the Colorado beetle who was an unwelcome guest. When I saw one of the bugs sitting on a potato leaf for the first time, I cried out to Grandpa, who happened to be with me, "Look, what a pretty beetle!" Grandpa grabbed the creature, threw it to the ground, and crushed it with his heel. I broke out in tears. "Why did you do that?" Grandpa explained to me patiently about those bugs, that they had nothing in mind but destroying our potatoes. So I learnt that pretty things can be as dangerous as ugly ones, and sometimes they had to be destroyed.

What I liked most was plucking the green peas with Granny. When we had gathered enough of them for our next meal, Granny and I sat in the sun on the bench behind the house. The bench came from the old church that stood on a slope above the village. When the church was renovated (before my time), Grandpa heaved one of its ancient benches, which were to be replaced, onto the neighbour's horse carriage and hauled it down the steep lane to the back of his house. The bench was hard, the seating surface too short, and the wood weathered. It was far from comfortable, but I loved the old thing, spending many hours sitting on it in the sun reading. But now we sat on it to peel the peas from their husks and let them roll into a chipped earthen bowl placed on the wobbly wooden table in front of the bench. I couldn't resist putting some of the peas in my mouth, for they had a sweet taste even when raw, and Granny warned me not to eat too many—otherwise I would get a tummy ache.

When I ignored her good advice and my tummy gave me pain, she would prepare a wormwood tea for me. I loathed its bitter taste, but it did help. Those were the happy days, when the bitterness lay in the herbal tea alone.

One evening the shopkeeper from across the road came to Grandpa for a shave. Clients would bother Grandpa at any time of the day from seven in the morning till eleven at night. As the barbershop was not much more than a wooden addition to the house, next to the living room with a connecting door, Grandpa couldn't pretend not to be in when he was. He never said no and took them on, even when they disturbed his meal or he was just going to bed. I was sitting on the waiting bench in the barbershop looking at the magazines when Grandpa came in with the client. Grandpa wanted to send me out, but the shopkeeper said, "Let her be. Why shouldn't she look at the magazines? There's no harm in that. Such a lovely little girl!"

When his stubble was gone and the cologne torture had been applied, he asked me if I would see him to his store across the road. There would be a sweet waiting for me. Grandpa saw no harm in that and let me go. When we got to the store, the shopkeeper led to me to the stockroom at the back, where he put a piece of chocolate in my mouth.

I was still chewing, looking curiously around in this room I had never seen before, when the man suddenly grabbed me, bent down to me, and pressed his lips on my throat. A smell of fresh cologne, old sweat, and stale wine hit my nostrils. I was more astonished at first than afraid, but my instincts told me something was not right. At the time I knew nothing about the facts of life, the bees and the trees, the boys and the girls, and what big men could do to small children in back rooms. Rising panic made me keep my eyes wide open, and I saw the little spectre, the one who sometimes put his finger to his mouth, dancing up and down in the air, changing colours at an alarming speed. Now I was really alarmed too, and I was afraid the guy was going to hurt me. His grip got tighter, and his breathing got harder. I tried to break loose, pretending to be playful and giggling so that he wouldn't get angry.

At the back of the stockroom lay the man's dog on a blanket, an old Alsatian who obviously didn't know what to make of the scene. He was wagging his tail and growling at the same time. The spectre rushed over to the dog and seemed to hit the animal's nose. The dog jumped up and rushed towards us, barking and grabbing the hem of my dress between his teeth, tearing it up. To him I was his master's attacker.

This brought the man to his senses. He let me go, and I fled, guided by the spectre that flew in front of me through the dark to see me home. I ran directly up the stairs to my bed. GrannyPa were sitting at the table in the living room, Granny knitting and Grandpa reading the paper. They heard my steps. Grandpa got up and called up the stairs.

"Emily, what are you doing up there?"

"Playing!" I managed to call back.

"Come down later to brush your teeth!"

"Yes!"

I didn't go down again. How could I tell GrannyPa what had happened? How could I explain the tear in my dress? Would the shopkeeper complain to GrannyPa because I had not properly thanked him for the chocolate? I felt terribly confused. I sat on my bed and cried as quietly as possible. Through my tears, I saw the spectre sitting next to me on the bed. His steady shine calmed me down. Suddenly I heard a whisper in my head, a soft voice talking to me without any outward sound. It was the spectre.

"Don't be afraid. The man will say nothing. You did nothing wrong."

"How do you know? Who are you? Why can you talk to me?"

"I am no one and everyone. I am a spirit watching over you from outside the material world, and you are one of the few humans who are able to see us spirits."

"Did you make the dog jump up so that I could get away? What's your name?"

"I am your friend. I will guide or follow you wherever you want me to go with you. I will help when necessary, but I will not make decisions for you. I do not have a name, but as you are a child and children need a name for everything, you can call me Lux."

"What kind of a name is that? Is it a foreign name?"

"In a way it is. It comes from an old language called Latin and it means 'light'."

"I like light," I murmured, suddenly feeling very tired, but I was calm and reassured again.

When GrannyPa came up to look for me, I was fast asleep.

In the morning I felt an itch at the base of my neck. I scratched. The itch came back at irregular intervals, especially when I looked across the road at the store. I never went to the store again, not alone and not even clinging to Grandpa's hand. I kept a close check on the cologne bottle, and when there was only a little of the liquid left so that a visit to the store was to be expected, I found excuses or went into hiding. On the spot where the itch had started, a dark scab developed. It didn't fall off like scabs usually do. On the contrary, it became hard and firmly embedded in the skin. Granny shook her head and put salve on it, which made no difference. They took me to the village doctor, but he could make nothing of the scab and advised Granny to continue with the salve.

"It looks like a tiny turtle's shell," Grandpa said. From then on he sometimes called me his "little turtle". I didn't like it, but I accepted it because he was my Grandpa who loved me, and I loved him and he meant no harm.

At the time none of us had the slightest idea that Grandpa's words were a prophecy. That one day I would become the Turtle Woman.

The Paradise Lost

Thirty years later I was leaning my head against the window of the big coach which was taking Anna and me on a tour around Ireland. Anna was the person I relied on most. She was a Polish woman in her fifties and had been living with me for ten years. She had wanted to move to Switzerland because her daughter and granddaughter lived close to Basel. What had started as employment became a close companionship over the years, a lifeline for me. She was my housekeeper, nurse, and surrogate mother all in one.

Flying from Zurich we had arrived in Dublin the morning of the day before and had gone on our first excursion in the afternoon—a bus tour in the centre of Dublin, including a visit to Trinity College. Though I found the Book of Kells very interesting and the library most impressive, I felt extremely uncomfortable and out of place as a mass tourist in a foreign city. After my life as a near recluse for nearly twenty years, this was so out of character for me. I could still not believe that I had let Mark talk me into going. But here I was, feeling ill at ease, especially with the pressure of the carapace on my body, all the same trying to concentrate on the tour guide's voice. We were on the road going south.

"Half an hour to Glendalough," the guide said, showering us with information about a medieval monastery founded by St Kevin in the early Middle Ages. I was moderately interested.

The rocking of the coach on the narrow road put me in a near-meditative state, making me not quite doze off, but get lost in thought. Shreds of memories fluttered through my mind, memories of my childhood—the happy times and the loss of the happiness.

***

When I look back now, I can see the incident in the stockroom as the first decisive break in my formerly peaceful and innocent existence. The incident was a secret that weighed on me for many years. The first person I ever talked to about it was my uncle Mark, three decades after it happened. I had never told GrannyPa, because I was afraid of how it would affect all our lives then. What if told them and they were angry with me? What if they got angry with the shopkeeper? What if they started a fight with the shopkeeper and couldn't go to the shop anymore? Where would Grandpa get his cologne then and Granny her groceries? There was another shop in the village, but it was further away and not so nice. GrannyPa didn't want to shop there; they only went there in cases of emergency.

Maybe I had done something wrong after all. Maybe the shopkeeper was just trying to be nice to me because he liked me, and he had overdone it a little bit. Maybe I should have told him gently I didn't like to be kissed by anyone except GrannyPa. Maybe then the dog would not have torn my dress. To GrannyPa I explained the tear by saying that the dog had got too excited when I was playing with him and that I was very sorry about the dress. Granny didn't scold me, and she mended the dress as best as she could. I would grow out of it soon anyway. Grandpa just grumbled something about the shopkeeper not having taught the dog to behave himself around small children and that I should keep away from the animal in the future. The shopkeeper came over the next day to apologize for his dog, saying I had teased the animal a bit too much and that the dog had meant no harm. I stood there hiding behind Grandpa's back. I knew the man was lying, because I hadn't teased the dog at all. But who would believe me? I was only a small child, and grown-ups always knew best what was right and wrong. Who would understand the discomfort and fear I had felt when the shopkeeper kissed me? Who would understand why I had struggled to free myself from the man's grip at all? On the other hand, why would the shopkeeper lie about a thing like that if there was nothing to it? It was all very confusing. So I kept quiet, and life went on as usual—except for me avoiding the shop.

The stock room incident cast a shadow over my last year with GrannyPa. Something had changed inside me. I would never be as carefree and trusting as before. On the outside there was the scab at the top of my back, a nuisance but not a pain, ugly to look at but covered by my clothes. Basically, things were as they used to be. I would wake up in the morning to the clatter of a horse's hooves, a sound I loved. One old farmer up the road still preferred driving to his fields on the horse cart instead of going on the tractor with his son. The horse, a docile brown mare, "a thoroughbred light cold-blood" as the farmer proudly stated, had grown old along with him, and he would keep her as long as she felt able to pull his cart or sometimes even take him for a short ride in the woods.

Grandpa was allowed to borrow the mare sometimes to go to the orchard he owned outside the village, when the apples and pears were ripe to be picked. He was very attached to the old long-stemmed trees, most of them Kläräpfels, though some experts told him to plant new short-stemmed varieties: they would bring better crops and would make picking easier. But Grandpa loved his old trees and stuck to them. They bore fruit ideal for cooking, preserving, and distilling schnapps. There was always an old wooden ladder waiting for him under one of the trees. He would let me climb up the ladder with him, and together we would pick the pears and apples, biting into the flesh of a few, especially the big ripe ones, though they had a tart taste to them and were nothing like the dessert fruit you buy in supermarkets nowadays.

The mare was waiting for us patiently, grazing between the trees unattached. She was a good horse, knowing her duties, and would never run away. She carried two saddle bags on her back without the saddle, for she came with us not to be ridden but to carry the fruit. Sometimes Grandpa would lift me onto her bare back, and she would carry me as well, while he led her by the bridle. One bag we would fill with the good fruit picked from the trees, the other with the fallen fruit picked from the ground. The fallen fruit must still be intact, without brown stains. It had to be taken directly to the distiller's to be made into schnapps. The good fruit went to the shop across the road, with Grandpa and the shopkeeper always haggling about the price, and some of it went to Granny, who made preserves or cooked it to a mush. The fresh hot mush we ate for dinner, with old bread fried in a pan with butter.

Once Grandpa took the horse to the smithy's down the road. The old farmer was sick, and Grandpa had offered to see to it that the horse got new shoes. The smithy's shop stood next to the village fountain on the main road where a smaller road forked off towards the castle on the hill. The main road led around the fountain in a sharp bend, and with the fountain blocking the view and the T-junction in the same place, the spot was dangerous for passing vehicles. Years later the fountain would be moved to a less perilous place and the main street was straightened. But that was after my time in the village.

The smithy did his work regardless of the occasional car collisions. Sometimes he couldn't even hear or see them, because he was so involved in the din his own work, hammering away on the metal for a horseshoe or a piece of iron fence, his face red and wet from the heat of the fire. I stood there watching him, wondering how anyone could do such work day in and day out without getting sick from the heat and deaf from the noise, even if he didn't burn himself on the red-hot iron. Grandpa stood outside holding the mare. The smithy lifted her feet one after the other, pulling away the old nails and shoes from her hooves. Didn't that hurt? I couldn't understand why a big strong animal like a horse would hold still for a treatment like that. If they did that to me, I would scream and struggle and kick, and the men wouldn't stand a chance! Grandpa explained to me that the hooves of horses were just horn which contained no nerves, so no pain could be felt. The animals were trained to tolerate the putting on and taking off of the horseshoes because they needed the shoes to protect their hooves, especially when going on a paved road.

"You wear shoes too, don't you?" said the smithy.

I did, but I would never let the smithy treat my feet like he treated the horses' feet!

Grandpa explained lots of things to me. I loved going for walks with him, especially up the hill to the ruin of the old castle. He would tell me the names of all the plants we met on the way, of all the butterflies and insects. Sometimes we would even catch a small frog in the grass or a salamander. He also told me the true story of the castle; it was called Farnsburg, and a bailiff had lived there in olden times, oppressing the people in the valleys below. One day the people fought back and ran up the hill to the castle to besiege and burn it. The bailiff gave up and had one very strong man carry him in a basket on his back down to Idylliken, where the bailiff managed to get on a horse and escape. The castle was stormed and destroyed, and there was a revolution. The country people broke away from the oppression of the haughty bourgeois of the City of Basel and declared themselves independent. The castle was never built up again. It served now as a viewpoint and picnic site for hikers. A circular staircase with well-trodden stone steps still led up to the old watchtower, from which you had a spectacular view on all sides over the valleys and villages below. Before the bailiffs, it had been a perfect vantage point for robber barons.

A short walk down from the castle there was a big farm with a restaurant. It was owned by two brothers, one tending to the farm and the other to the restaurant. In the summer you could sit outside on a terrace and look over the green hills. Sometimes Grandpa treated me to an apple juice. Afterwards we would visit the stables and the pastures, watching the cows graze and ruminate and the pigs slurp their food from troughs, squeaking and waggling their curled tails. Chicken ran freely in the compound, the cock watching over them attentively. Once he even attacked me when I got too close to his hens, fluttering up from the ground and pushing his claws against me. I shrieked, and Grandpa had to shoo the cocky cock away.

***

The coach came to a stop in a huge parking lot, which was still nearly empty. Our guide had insisted on departing early. "We want to be ahead of the posse," he said. Obviously we were. The visitor's centre had only just opened. The guide's name was Niall. He was fortyish, with dark hair, grey temples, a slightly beaky nose, and a strong chin. And he was very eloquent. Driving and talking smoothly at the same time for hours didn't seem to be a problem to him. He was solely responsible for this tour. He had given us all badges with our first names, which we were to wear the whole time. He was wearing one too. We were a big group—over forty people—all Americans and Australians, except for us two Swiss ladies. That is to say, Anna wasn't really Swiss. She was Polish, but she had been living in Switzerland for many years, ten of them with me.

I descended the steep stairs of the coach clumsily. Anna went ahead of me, holding her hand up in case I needed support. Niall watched and held up his hand too. I ignored both of them and managed to get down on my own. From behind I felt the eyes of our fellow travellers on my back. My embarrassment became nearly unbearable, but I had sworn to myself and Mark that I would pull through this.

I caught a glimpse of Niall's face when my feet touched the ground. It wore a slight frown, and there was a curious speculative expression in his eyes. I walked away with Anna as fast as I could towards the entrance to the visitors' centre, where we had a quarter of an hour to look at the presentation about the historic site of Glendalough and the souvenir shop. Afterwards a middle-aged woman took us on a walking tour, feeding us with more information than we could possibly digest.

When we entered the actual site I felt it for the first time—the welling up of a strange energy that floated me like a soft small wave. There was a kind of magic and a mystic whispering in the air. It was in the incredible beauty of the valley—not only in the sight of the woody hills, the green meadows, and the clear water of the two small lakes, but even more in the spiritual quality of the beauty. It lay in the Celtic crosses on the graveyard, weather-beaten stone relicts from very old times, and in the little church built entirely of grey stone, nearly intact after many centuries. I stood in the half-darkness of the church, my nose twitching at the musty smell inside, my mind trying to pick up the guide's explanations. I found it impossible because of an unexpected distraction. Under the church's roof small shiny shapes appeared, becoming slowly visible to my eyes. Lux was dancing amongst them, beaming in bright yellow. I had nearly forgotten about Lux, because I had felt so miserable for so long, and especially for the last two days. There they were—the glow worms from my childhood who had lit up the dark staircase in GrannyPa's home for me! I stood in wonder, my face turned up to the ceiling, my heart giving a merry little jolt.

I nearly missed the next stage of the tour. Anna had to pull me away by my sleeve after all the others had left the church. Stepping out into the sunlight, I noticed that each grave had its own spirit. Some of the shiny shapes were sitting on the tombstones, some on the crosses. Suddenly I felt my spirits lifted, my mood rising up from the despair and confusion, and I understood that Mark had been right to suggest this trip. Something began to touch my inner core, penetrating the hard shell that encased me.

Anna and I got back to the bus ahead of the others. Niall already stood there, talking into his mobile, obviously complaining about something. He got off the phone when we approached him. I was so uplifted that I felt the impulse to uplift someone else, to chase away another person's bad mood.

"Are you stressed out?" I asked.

He just let out a groan.

"But why? You are lucky to drive such nice people around."

This was one of my first attempts at joking. Anna looked at me in wonder. She had never seen me so outgoing.

Niall frowned. "Give me a break on that one!" he said.

I was taken aback and felt somewhat offended. I looked at Anna and saw a big grin on her face. My feeling of offence dissolved. She made me climb into the bus, and when we were installed in our seats, she whispered into my ear, "I like the guy. Here's a man who speaks his mind!"

She was right on that one.

The coach rocked on towards our next stop, which would be New Ross. Again my thoughts led me back down memory lane, to my village and the old house which had been pulled down in the meantime to be replaced by a modern block. I would never get over that loss and how it had come about.

***

One day Margrit, the baker's daughter, came looking for me. She had Robi in tow, the butcher's son, and Vreni, a girl with black teeth who lived up the road in one of the "lesser" areas. GrannyPa didn't like Vreni so much. On the other hand, it wasn't the child's fault that her parents were no-goods. We four children were about the same age. The other three found me on the church bench at the back of the house, reading one of Grandpa's magazines. Robi looked around the corner to check if any grown-ups were close by, acting very secretive. Then he whispered into my ear, "My father is slaughtering a pig today. Would you like to come and watch?"

I knew I was not allowed to go near the small slaughterhouse behind the butcher's shop. Also, the notion of a pig being slaughtered didn't appeal to me. I thought of the pigs on the farm up the mountain, especially the rosy piglets, and felt sorry for them. On the other hand, I was curious what was inside a pig.

"Are you a sport or not?"

Robi's provocation got the better of me. I left my magazine and followed the others to the slaughterhouse. We took the overgrown lane behind the houses, fighting our way through bushes, mounting a few fences, and finally creeping up from behind to the red-brick building which was the slaughterhouse. We peeped through the windows. The pig and the butcher and the farmer who had sold him the pig were already in place. The pig, a young gelded boar, obviously had a premonition about the fate reserved for him. He broke free and ran around the room, a piece of rope around his neck. He squealed in panic. The men tried to catch him, which they eventually did. The farmer straddled the pig, pulling the rope around his neck, and the butcher held a metal tube to the head of the animal. He pulled a trigger and the pig fell down, twitched for a few seconds, and lay still.

I felt horror and fascination at the same time, pity and curiosity fighting each other in my breast.

The men now knotted a rope around the dead pig's hind legs and pulled it up so that it hung from a beam on the ceiling. They cut its throat to let the blood flow into a basin below. The bloodless carcass was hauled into a big vat filled with very hot water, floating there for a while. Then they pulled it out again and started scraping the skin of the animal with iron instruments to make the bristles come off. This took a while. I wondered when the cutting open would begin.

Meanwhile GrannyPa had missed me. Grandpa was looking for me in all the places I could usually be found. He was really getting worried, until someone gave him the tip that four children had been seen creeping up behind the butcher's shop. There he found me, pulled my ear (though not very hard), and gave Robi a piece of his mind about seducing an innocent girl to watch a brutality like the slaughtering of a pig, which was a sight reserved only for hardened grown-ups.

I never got to see the insides of a pig being taken out live in real time. Much later, after the invention of computers, I once tried to watch such a scene on a film on the Internet. I didn't go through with it.

The summer I turned seven I was supposed to start school. The long summer holidays were coming to an end, and I was excited at the prospect of school. Granny had gone with me to a seamstress in Gelterkinden, the main village of our district, to order a few dresses for me. Though she was a teacher of handiwork herself, dressmaking was not her strong point. Her pride in me demanded something better, clothes made by a real expert. The seamstress showed me catalogues with grown-up dresses; I could choose three. With a sure instinct for the unusual, I chose the three most elaborate designs. The seamstress took my measurements, saying she would add a centimetre or two because I was growing fast. Granny agreed.

The day came when my dresses were ready. Granny took me by the hand, and we walked the two kilometres to Gelterkinden on a hot August day. My birthday would be tomorrow, and I was supposed to wear the best of the three dresses for the little party GrannyPa had planned for me. I had invited Margrit, Vreni, and even Robi, whom GrannyPa had forgiven the affair with the pig. The butcher had made his son apologize to GrannyPa. Granny baked a cake, and Grandpa bought seven small candles to put on the cake. I was very excited and couldn't wait to see my presents, but they were safely locked up in the cupboard—except for the dresses, which, of course, couldn't have been made secretly and without my cooperation.

When Granny and I got home, hot and tired from carrying the bags with the new dresses all the way from Gelterkinden, Grandpa was standing in front of the house. His face was grim and pale.

"Nelly is here," he whispered into Granny's ear.

"Who is Nelly?" I asked.

Before they knew how to answer my question the door opened and a strange woman stepped out into the little front garden. The first thing I noticed about her was her eyes. They were green and wide, set under dark brows with a butterfly shape like mine. The woman and I looked at each other. I let go of Granny's hand and ran away and hid in the stable. There I sat on the dirty floor, utterly afraid and confused, though

I didn't understand why. That is to say, I began to understand, but I didn't want to. The bubbly cow and the goats were there, turning their muzzles towards my face, licking the tears from my cheeks with their transparent tongues. It felt like tiny soap bubbles bursting on my face. Lux sat on my knee.

"This woman is my mother, isn't she?"

Lux confirmed it. He knew all the questions and thoughts that were tumbling around in my mind. Where did she come from? Where had she been all those years? A mother is supposed to be there, or at least to ask about her child, and if she doesn't, she must be dead. Why wasn't she dead? Why did she turn up all of a sudden? Why did GrannyPa never say that I had a mother? I never missed her. I don't want her now. We did just fine without her. WHY?

"This was bound to happen. It is your destiny," Lux said. "It may be hard for you, but every human being should know where he or she comes from. Knowing who your parents are is part of it. So far, you had this question buried in your mind, avoiding it. Now you have to deal with it, difficult as it may be. Also there is still the question of your father. Ask Granny!"

Slowly I got up, tiptoed through the back door into the kitchen, and pressed my ear on the door to the living room. I heard angry voices and understood bits of the continuing argument.

"You can't just take her away! You've never come to visit, never cared!" Grandpa shouted.

". . . My child! You made me leave her behind . . ." This must be Nelly.

Sobbing sounds. Then Granny's voice louder than I had never heard from her.

"She is happy here. She belongs here. You can come and visit if you want to see her!"

I realized they were talking about me, fighting about me. It was unbearable. I flung the door open. They were all sitting around the dining table. I rushed towards Granny and sat on her lap.

"Go away!" I shrieked at the strange woman who had crashed into our peaceful existence without any advance warning and was putting a claim on me without even asking.

I clung to Granny, burying my head on her shoulder. Nelly started crying. Granny and I cried. Grandpa tried not to cry, with no success. It was the worst thing that had ever happened to me.

"See how unhappy you are making her!" Grandpa said angrily to Nelly.

"This is all your fault! You chased me away! You had no heart for your own daughter!"

What was she talking about? Grandpa was the most soft-hearted person I knew. He always had a heart for me. How could she talk to him like that?

Suddenly Granny's fist pounced on the table. Grandpa, Nelly, and I went stiff with surprise. Gentle quiet Granny, who seldom talked and hardly ever talked back, was losing her temper.

"Shut up, you two!" she said with an authority she had otherwise reserved for her schoolgirls.

"Don't you see how upsetting this is for the child? Don't you give a damn about her feelings? Out with you! Leave me alone with her. There's some explaining to do!"

Grandpa took Nelly by the arm and led her through the kitchen to the back of the house. Granny put me down on the floor and made me sit on the sofa next to her. Wiping my tears with one of her lily-white hankies, she began with the explaining.

Granny said Grandpa wouldn't agree with her telling me everything, but she felt she had to. For once she would go against his wishes. But I mustn't think this was my fault. It was their problem if they didn't agree on something, not mine. I deserved to know the truth. Grandpa meant well in his own way. He wanted to protect me from the truth, but Granny thought I was old enough for the truth, and new circumstances demanded that she told me what had been going on with my mother and why she had never come to visit me.

I cannot remember exactly what Granny told me then, what details were revealed later when I was older, and what pieces I was able to put together myself. Anyway, here is the essence of what happened, the seed of evil from which came the troubles I was to see in the following years.

It all began when Nelly finished school at sixteen. She was GrannyPa's only child. "I had four miscarriages after Nelly," Granny said, and she explained to me about miscarriages—that the little babies she carried had died very early while still in her belly and had come out dead and too small to live anyway. I felt very sorry for those little babies and that GrannyPa had lost four children and Nelly four little brothers or sisters. Nelly, as the only living child, was the apple of GrannyPa's eyes. They were proud of her because she was a lovely girl and clever in school. Nelly had a high clear voice and loved to sing. She sang with the church choir and after school. She declared that she wanted to become a professional singer. Grandpa told her she had a bee in her bonnet. A girl should learn something solid and useful for the house, because she would get married one day, and a man didn't want a wife with fancy ideas about being a star, but a good housewife and mother.

"This is 1968 and not the Middle Ages," Nelly had said. "I have talent. Even the music teacher told me so, and he will help me to get into music school in Basel."

Grandpa got furious and went to the music teacher to give him a piece of his mind. How dare he put such a gigantic bee in the girl's bonnet? She was to become a seamstress; that was an honest and solid profession for a young woman. Grandpa got Nelly an apprenticeship with a seamstress in Gelterkinden, the very same who had made my new dresses, and Nelly had to comply. She never forgave Grandpa, and from then on there was war between father and daughter. Grandpa was always reminding her that she was a minor and had to do what she was told. As long as she put her feet under his table, he was calling the shots.

After a year or so, Nelly started going out more and more, even when Grandpa ordered her to stay home, and she started staying away for whole nights.

"She got out of control," Granny said. "I tried to call them both to their senses. I begged them to keep the peace, to love and understand each other. It was no use. It was a terrible time for all of us. We all suffered, each in his or her own way."

Grandpa called Nelly a harlot when she stayed out and shouted that no decent man would ever respect her. She was ruining her chances for a good marriage. One day GrannyPa found out where Nelly spent some of her nights. She was seen kissing Patrick, a boy from the village, a little older than Nelly and something of an outcast. He was a handsome boy with blond curls, a freckled nose, and peculiar light grey eyes. His eyes were almost silvery and seemed to look right through you. Patrick's mother had the same silvery eyes, but her hair was the colour of dark copper, and she was an outcast too. She was a foreigner and a Catholic on top of that, which in itself was a reason for suspicion in our very evangelical Idylliken. Her name was Fiona, and what kind of a name was that in a Protestant Swiss village? "She is Irish," people used to say in an undertone that suggested that being Irish was something really suspicious. Fiona and her son Patrick sometimes went to the Roman Catholic church in Gelterkinden on Sundays, not to our little Protestant church on the hill.

Fiona had come to the village as the wife of a local farmer's fourth son, named Paul. He had gone abroad because he couldn't expect to inherit anything from his father; the farm would go to his eldest brother. He ended up in Ireland, on some very wild island called Inis Mór off the west coast in the Bay of Galway, where they spoke a strange language called Gaelic. There he worked for a widowed farmer and married the farmer's daughter, Fiona. They married secretly and only in a civil ceremony, because she was a Catholic and he a Protestant, and no priest or pastor they asked was willing to marry them in church.

When the old farmer died, Paul and Fiona sold the farm on the island, because they could barely make a living from it, and they moved to Paul's native village in Switzerland, where they hoped to find another farm. But the price of property had gone up, and their money bought them only a cabin half-hidden in the woods outside Idylliken. Paul did a lot of repairs to the cabin and made it habitable. Fiona was used to simple ways and hard work. All she wanted was to make a life with Paul. They both worked as day labourers, he in the stables and fields of the local farmers and she doing chores around households and gardens, occasionally also helping with the harvests.

"I liked Fiona," Granny said. "Not many people did, out of sheer superstition. They said she had eyes like she was seeing ghosts all the time."

"Granny, I can see ghosts!" I hadn't meant to tell; it just slipped out of me.

"Dear child, you have such a vivid imagination!"

I opened my mouth to protest that it was not imagination but the truth, that I could really see ghosts. But then I sensed Lux signalling to me to let it go. It would be too much for Granny to understand right now. She was preoccupied with other things. Maybe some other time, but the time never came, because later I was preoccupied with other things, and one day GrannyPa left this world without me being prepared for their loss.

When Fiona's son was born, he had his mother's eyes, and she named him Pádraic. He was generally called Patrick by everyone else, because people couldn't pronounce "Pádraic". Granny wrote the name down for me on a piece of paper. Fiona had spelled it out for her when the boy was small. Fiona was a clever woman, Granny said. She spoke Gaelic, which is spoken in Ireland and Scotland, and English as well, and she picked up our local dialect really fast. She also knew a lot about herbs and healing, which made her seem all the more suspicious to the village people who called her "the witch". Nonetheless, some of the local women secretly went to see her when they had "female troubles" and didn't want to consult the doctor. Fiona also knew a lot about helping with the birth of animals and was sometimes called to the stables in difficult cases. She gave birth to her son all by herself in the little cabin.

Paul and Fiona did all right. They had a modest but sufficient income. Fiona kept a few chickens in a pen and grew vegetables in her garden like Granny. Patrick was good in school, but the other boys always teased him and played practical jokes on him. When they grew older, the boys especially didn't like that the girls liked Patrick, even if the girls wouldn't admit to it. They knew their brothers and fathers would disapprove. When Nelly decided to like Patrick and act on it, Grandpa's worst fears were confirmed.

"I could understand Nelly," said Granny, "though I didn't approve either. She was too young, and I didn't see a future for her and Patrick. I hated the thought of her spending nights in the woods with a boy of eighteen, and she only just seventeen and both nowhere in their lives. He was an apprentice with the smithy and she a reluctant seamstress. What kind of basis was that for a successful future?"

Also, Patrick had already lost his father. Paul, unhappy with his status as an underprivileged farmhand instead of a proud farmer, had spent more and more time in the local pubs. Often he left a big part of his wages there. He was the kind who got whiny when drunk, and sometimes Fiona had to pick him up from the pub when the landlord wanted to get rid of the wimp with his head in the beer puddles on the table. One night when Paul was staggering home on his own, he must have lost his balance on the bridge over the river, probably leaning over the railing to spit out the contents of his stomach. He was found in the morning. Whether he had died from drowning or a broken neck was difficult to say. Patrick was fifteen at the time. Fiona would have liked to go back to her native Island, but for her son's sake she stayed on, thinking he was too old to be uprooted from the place where he was born. Also he didn't speak much English, let alone Gaelic.

When Nelly and Patrick became lovers, Grandpa was sure his daughter was doing it just to scorn him. Why else would she pick the least eligible boy he could imagine? Granny didn't see it that way. She felt that Nelly and Patrick were really in love. Granny went to see Fiona, and the two women cried together. Neither of them agreed with the ways things were going; the sin and the risk of this relationship were heavy burdens on them. For Fiona the stress was mainly about the sin of being unchaste, while for Granny it was more about the risk of an untimely pregnancy. Unfortunately, Granny's fears were well founded. Soon Nelly missed her period. Fiona knew herbs that would take care of the problem, but of course that would be an even bigger sin. After all, it would be her own grandchild she would be murdering. Patrick said he was prepared to marry Nelly at once, but as they were both still minors they couldn't do it without the parent's consent. Grandpa flatly refused.

"The groom a no-good and the mother-in-law a foreign witch! No way! We'll solve the problem differently!"

There were ugly scenes between the parents and the daughter and between the parents themselves. There was also an ugly scene between Patrick and Grandpa, which would have ended in a fist fight if Granny hadn't thrown herself between the two men. Grandpa threatened Patrick with the police if he ever came near his daughter again.

Grandpa decided to send Nelly away to his youngest sister Julie, who lived in Rapperswil on the Lake of Zurich. There Nelly was supposed to continue her training as a seamstress with her aunt, who was a seamstress herself, and to help with the household and have a discreet delivery when her time came. Julie was married to a physician with a private practice, which was ideal under the circumstances. They had a ten-year-old son named Mark.

Within a week Nelly disappeared from Idylliken. GrannyPa took her to Rapperswil on the train. Grandpa told her she was to keep a low profile and not contact Patrick, and that nobody in Idylliken must know about her "problem".

"Our family has always been held in high esteem. You are not going to ruin our good name!"

Grandpa knew he could count on Julie, who shared his attitude and promised to watch Nelly closely. Nelly, worn out from sadness and helplessness, was resigned to her situation and did what she was ordered to do. She spent the following months under the stern regime of her aunt, her pregnancy medically monitored by the uncle. Her only comfort was Mark, a gentle boy with unusual insight for a child his age. They played games together and talked a lot, though

Aunt Julie wasn't too pleased with her son getting so close to a "fallen" woman. On the other hand, she was not heartless and could see that Nelly suffered. So Julie tried to keep a balance between being loyal to her brother and empathic to her niece, but not too empathic.

I was born on a hot August day in a discreet private clinic on the so called "Gold Coast" of the Lake of Zurich. Julie's husband had pulled a few strings to get Nelly a bed there. I was registered as a child born from an unknown father, and Julie was appointed as my and Nelly's guardian. Nelly gave me the name of Emily. Nelly was eighteen and would become of age only at twenty. At the time children from single mothers automatically had a legal guardian appointed to them.

When Nelly was in bed after giving birth, GrannyPa came to see her and the baby.

"We fell in love with you at first sight," Granny said.

Nelly begged her parents in tears that they would let Patrick see her and his little daughter. Granny made Grandpa leave the room and took her daughter's hand.

Nelly knew at once that something was wrong. As gently as possible, Granny broke the news to her that Patrick had left them. A few weeks ago he had apparently gotten into a brawl when out with the boys. In spite of GrannyPa's attempt to keep the family affair a secret, there were rumours going around. Some of the boys had teased Patrick until he lost his temper. When he didn't get home that night, Fiona went looking for him. She found him in the county hospital in Liestal, the capital of the county of Basel-Land. Patrick had an ugly wound on his head and a cracked skull, and he was in a coma. The boys who had been out with him knew nothing, had seen nothing, and weren't very forthcoming with information at all. The police investigation led to no conclusive results. Fiona spent most of her time at her son's bedside during the following weeks. Pádraic never woke up again.

"Good riddance!" Grandpa said when he heard the news. After that Granny wouldn't speak to him for a long time.

Fiona buried her son in the Catholic graveyard in Gelterkinden. Granny was the only person with her. Fiona gave Granny a copy of Pádraic's birth certificate and a family snapshot of the boy, Paul, and herself, taken shortly before Paul had died.

"For the child," she said, "when she is old enough."

She also gave Granny a document with the power of attorney to sell her cabin.

"Money also for the child. I go back to my home soon. Look after my chickens. Thank you for being friend to me."

Two days later she was gone. Granny asked the farmer next door to pick up the chickens, which he gladly did. She sold the cabin and all that Fiona had left behind to an Italian worker who wanted to settle down in Idylliken, and she put the money in a bank account under my name. She did all this without consulting Grandpa. For once Grandpa didn't insist on his right as the patriarch to make all the decisions. As to the money, it even seemed to mollify him a bit.

"So she did have some decency after all," he muttered, meaning Fiona.

Granny gave him another spell of the silent treatment.

On that memorable day when my mother turned up unexpectedly, Granny showed me the copy of the birth certificate and the photo for the first time. She would keep them for me, she said. I could look at them any time I wanted to, and I should tell no one. She was afraid Nelly might take the documents and never hand them over to me. I should keep this a secret, she said. Even Grandpa didn't know she had the birth certificate and the photo. I looked at the certificate, the dates and names on it, and Granny helped me spell out the name and birthplace of my Irish grandmother, which was Fiona from Kilmurvy on the Island of Inis Mór, or Inishmore in English.

"Maybe one day you will meet her," Granny said, "if she is still alive."

"Granny," I said, "why did my mother go away when I was born? Didn't she want me?"

Granny sighed. "No, darling, that wasn't the problem. She fell into a deep post-natal depression and had to go to a clinic for a long time. She was so sick she couldn't take care of you. So Grandpa and I came to get you, because Julie said she couldn't keep you. We felt very sad and guilty because of the terrible things that had happened. Grandpa did too, even if he didn't want to admit it. We wanted at least to give you all the happiness we could."

"What is a poss-natel depression?"

"When a woman is very sad after her child is born. Some women have that, even without a good reason. Nelly did have a reason, more than one. When she got out of the clinic, she disappeared without telling anyone where she went, not us and not her aunt and uncle. I think she should have told us where she was for your sake, even if she didn't want to see us. And she should have come back earlier, not just after seven long years."

Later my mother told me she had only wanted to see her parents again when she could prove to them that she was able to make a success of herself. And when she had someone at her side who would help her. That someone was Kurt, my stepfather-to-be.

Old Pains

On the road to New Ross, Niall prepared his passengers for the visit to the historic sailing ship *Dunbrody,* which had taken many Irish emigrants to New York from the middle of the nineteenth century on. Those of the group who didn't prefer to take a nap were captivated by his vivid account of the Great Famine, all delivered with his eyes on the road, his hands on the steering wheel, and his mouth on the microphone.

"It started in 1844 and got really bad from 1845 on. Imagine yourself to be a father of seven children, the eighth on the way. You stand on the border of your potato field, which provides for your whole diet, apart from an occasional cabbage, an egg per week per person, and a fish or two when you have the time to go fishing and are lucky enough to catch one. So you stand there and your field stinks. You dig up a potato and it's rotten. So is the next one and all the other ones too. The fields and vegetable gardens of your neighbours stink as well. The potatoes have caught the Blight, which is a very contagious potato disease. The Blight was all over Europe, but no other country depended so much on the potato as Ireland. You belong to that third of the Irish population who live mainly on potatoes, so you can imagine what it does to your daily menu. Soon you try to live on grass soup or you go begging. Your wife gives birth to an undernourished baby with no chance of survival, because the mother doesn't have enough milk. You are the tenant of a small farm, owing money to the landlord whether you can pay or not. The landlord sends his middleman to extract from you the last bit of dough or any goods he can find, because he gets his share of what he robs from you.

"Ireland is still under the rule of the English Crown, which doesn't do much to feed the mouths of its starving Irish subjects. Anyway, to some English the best Irishman is a dead Irishman, with the Irishwoman and the Irish child on the side. The gracious Queen Victoria parts with £2,000 of her modest fortune to buy some grub for the starving. Even the Ottoman Sultan Abdülmecid, a Muslim, is prepared to donate more to the needy Christians in the West of Europe; he offers £10,000. The English sovereign Victoria, as a good Christian, tells him to reduce that sum to a tenth; she couldn't bear the humiliation of letting a foreigner give more than she did. So the Sultan secretly sends three ships full of food to Ireland, which the English unsuccessfully try to block. At the same time, ships full of Irish agricultural products and cattle are exported to England to be consumed by the already overfed English gentry. From 1845 to 1852, Ireland loses about a fourth of her population. One million die; a few hundred thousand scrape together the fare for a sailing ship to America, Canada, or Australia. They are squashed into the bellies of the boats as steerage under less than comfortable conditions, to put it mildly. Not enough water, not enough to eat, no fresh air, no lavatories, no privacy. Not all the poor wretches who make it onto a ship make it to their destination. Many are buried at sea on the way. A visit to the famine ship *Dunbrody* will give you an idea of what the Irish version of a cruise around the world meant in those days.

"Speaking of lavatories—they are to the left where I let you out on the pier. Get your ticket at the booth; it's already paid for. I'll pick you up in an hour and a half, not one minute later. See ye!"

Descending into the hold of the *Dunbrody* down a steep flight of stairs not much more than a ladder was no easy exercise for me, but I was determined to make it. The visit to the ship proved to be a most impressive experience. Just looking at the narrow bunks in the half-darkness gave me the shudders. Two local women acted the parts of *Dunbrody* passengers based on real life stories, one a first-class and one a steerage traveller. I climbed the stairs back up sideways, with Anna pushing a little from below, proud of myself for beginning to live up to the challenges of this trip.

The next challenge was a short tour of Waterford. Walking was not my strong point. If I wasn't careful, the rim of my shell rubbed constantly on my upper thighs. I had to take short steps, and I could hardly keep up with the others. A local guide pointed out the remains of the Viking strongholds. The Vikings had pillaged the countryside regularly from the eighth century on, after sailing and rowing up the rivers in their flat boats, and they founded the City of Waterford as a fortified base in the ninth century. The famous Round Tower still stands intact, a carapace no medieval cannon could breach.

My mood, which had lightened up considerably since Glendalough, was sinking again. I began to brood about my own carapace and wonder if there would be any means of getting rid of it one day. Back at the hotel I decided to skip dinner. Anna asked if she should keep me company, but I refused. So she went alone and obviously had a good time, for she came to the room quite late. I was lying on the bed in my clothes with the TV on, trying to concentrate on a rerun of "Britain's Got Talent". She brought me a sandwich and a piece of lemon cake. I took a few bites of each with a cup of tea she made from the electric kettle and the teabags deposited on the sideboard.

"I spoke to the guide," she said. "He intercepted me in the lobby in front of the elevator and insisted I had a beer with him in the bar. He had a question to ask me. It soon became clear that he was not interested in my charms but in yours."

"You must be joking!" I said, getting somewhat angry because I thought it was a bad joke.

"I'm serious. He tried to be subtle, but subtlety is not really in his nature, I think. Anyway, I took the liberty of telling him you were a writer looking for inspiration for a new book and that I would be grateful if he kept this to himself. It wasn't difficult to guess the questions he didn't dare to ask. I have a feeling he will try to talk to you directly."

"Why should he? I'm sure it's just curiosity about why I have such a funny figure and move so clumsily. Next time tell him to go to hell!"

"Tell him that yourself!" Anna was unmoved by my bad temper.

We went to bed. I couldn't go to sleep for a long time, trying to remember what life had been like when I was still an agile young girl moving around normally and asking myself how it could have happened that I turned into a two-legged, clumsy turtle within such a short time.

***

Kurt. It had a lot to do with Kurt, my mother's husband, my stepfather, later my adopted father against my will. It had not been Kurt's fault alone; there were further circumstances as well. Some had to do with my mother, some with the death of GrannyPa, and some probably with my own inclination to hole up if I felt bad. The whole thing took on the form of a vicious circle I didn't know how to escape.

When my mother came to see GrannyPa and me for the second time, she had a man with her. He was quite good-looking and wore a nice suit and a silk tie. Nelly presented him proudly. "This is Kurt, my fiancé. He's a lawyer and just opened his own office."

Kurt went out of his way to be friendly. He brought me a box of chocolates and GrannyPa a big bunch of flowers. In view of Granny's two flower gardens, the one on the side of the house and the smaller one in front, this was not the best choice for a gift, but it was accepted as a gesture. GrannyPa were duly impressed by

Kurt's manner and appearance, but they had their reservations because they felt he might be a threat, reinforcing Nelly's position. Which proved to be exactly the case. After coffee and cake and the formal exchange of niceties, I was sent out to play behind the house. "We have to discuss some grown-up stuff, little turtle."

As I left the room through the kitchen very slowly, trying to pick up some of the conversation through the not quite closed door, I heard Nelly say, "Why do you call her that? What kind of a nickname is that for a child?"

"Well, as you say, it's just a nickname!" Grandpa sounded irritated. "What's the fuss? There are more important things to discuss than a nickname which is meant as an endearment. She likes it."

This wasn't exactly true. I just didn't mind it coming from Grandpa. But who was Nelly to tell him what he was supposed to call me? How dare she interfere with our life? Someone in the room got up and closed the door to the kitchen. I went to the church bench and sat on it for a long time, dangling my legs. I sensed trouble lying ahead. I looked at Lux sitting on my knee, turning him for comfort. Nelly was trying to interfere, maybe even take me away from GrannyPa, from my home, from my village. The man was here to help her. Lux knew and I knew. I cried silently. Lux signalled he would always be with me. They couldn't take him away.

It happened as we had feared, GrannyPa and I. Granny told me later what had been discussed in the room while I waited on the bench. The four had gotten into a heated argument, GrannyPa claiming they had been looking after me since I was born, and Nelly hadn't cared. Nelly said that she had cared, but she had been sick at first, and later she had been afraid to come back for me because Grandpa had been so hard on her, and she wouldn't have known how to look after me all by herself, living in the city and trying to make it there.

Apparently she had gone to Basel after the clinic. Social services had helped her get a room in flat-sharing community and a job of some sort in a residence for senior citizens, working in the kitchen and cleaning. She went to evening school for secretarial training and got her diploma and then an office job with an insurance company. A colleague at work motivated her to do an audition for a big choir in Basel where he sang himself, saying they were always in need of good young voices. The audition went well. She was taken on and soon got all the small soprano solo parts, the big ones, of course, being sung by professionals in the concerts.

After four years on her own, Nelly had made a success of herself in every way, except for men. She couldn't get over Patrick for a long time. Also, she was still not ready to deal with the past. For another three years she kept putting the moment off where she would have to confront her parents and me. Then she met Kurt and finally felt up to the challenge.

Kurt had just finished his training as a solicitor. He gained Nelly's trust, listening to her life story and confirming for her the injustice of it all—that she had been treated badly and without regard for her own feelings and wishes. He would stand by her and help her see that justice was done. She would be his first case to take to court, if necessary, and he wouldn't charge her. A few days later he took her to dinner and proposed to her. She accepted. So when she turned up with him in Idylliken, she was proudly wearing a small diamond ring. GrannyPa and I understood that against Nelly on her own we would have stood a chance, but not against Nelly and that lawyer fiancé of hers. They both had a point to prove—she to repair the wrong which had been done to her, he that he would win his first case.

The case never went to court. Nelly and Kurt married soon, Nelly insisting on a religious ceremony in our little church on the hill. After all, she was a village girl who had come out on top, in spite of the past, in spite of the shame and the covering up and the gossip and the death of her first love, and she would show them all. She did. She wore a white wedding gown, simple but costly-looking, with a lacy veil and a short train I was to carry. I also wore white, a dress borrowed from the seamstress in Gelterkinden who had made it for her younger daughter a few years back. Kurt looked handsome in a black cutaway with a silver bow tie.

By the standards of our village the wedding party was big. There were GrannyPa in clothes I had never seen them in before, Grandpa in a dark ill-fitting suit and Granny in a long blue skirt with a frilly white blouse. There was Aunt Julie with her doctor husband and Mark, now a young man of seventeen, cousin to Nelly and uncle in the second degree to me. There were a few other relatives, most unknown to me. The baker, the butcher, and the farmer next door were there with their families. There were city people from Basel, friends of Kurt and Nelly. A few members of Nelly's choir sang two elaborate pieces from "an oratory by Mendelssohn", as Nelly explained to me. I didn't know what Mendelssohn was or what oratory meant.

Many village people who had not been invited came to watch the wedding party outside the church, some even sneaking inside to follow the ceremony. I overheard two village hags whispering that it was a disgrace that the bride dared wear white, a colour reserved for pure girls, and her child born out of wedlock too, and the choir singing pieces by a Jewish composer. Morals were decaying and rules disrespected of late, even in Idylliken. "They will corrupt us in no time, you'll see!" At least, they said, the groom seemed to be of the presentable and decent kind, Nelly was more than lucky in view of her shady past, and one could only hope that this marriage would last, also for the sake of the child, who got the chance now to grow up in decent circumstances. After all, it was not the girl's fault she had been produced by an irresponsible adolescent mother and the son of foreign witch.

They must have seen me standing close by and obviously didn't care if I overheard or not. I was close to tears. Lux snuggled up to my neck;

otherwise I would have broken out in sobs. The scab on my back began to itch, but of course I couldn't even think of scratching it with my white dress covering the sore spot and everyone watching. Recently the spot had grown somewhat, spreading sideways and downwards. It seemed to grow every time after an attack of itching.

From GrannyPa's faces I could tell they weren't really enjoying the occasion either. On one hand this wedding did give them back some of the lost family honour; on the other hand it meant that they had to let me go. Nelly and Kurt would pick me up after a short honeymoon in the Canary Islands. GrannyPa and I had one week to say goodbye. Of course, I could still come and visit them, or they me, but it wouldn't be the same. I dreaded the day when Nelly and Kurt would come to take me away to the city. The fact that they could offer me a bathroom with a tub and water closet, plus central heating instead of a small wood stove which never gave off enough heat in winter, was no consolation to me. Also I hardly knew my own mother, and I knew my new father even less. Kurt was friendly enough to me—overfriendly sometimes; I felt he tried too hard. His big brown eyes made him look like a devoted dog at first sight, but there was a hint of calculation in the way he let his heavy lids droop when watching someone. It made me feel uneasy when he looked at me.

Nelly insisted I call Kurt Papa. She was to be addressed as Mama. Nelly was convinced we would be a happy family.

***

Anna woke me up in the morning; I hadn't had enough sleep and was in a rotten mood. Her suggestion that Niall might try to talk to me had made me edgy. I decided to avoid him if possible.

After breakfast we were on the road again. The first item on the agenda was a visit to the Waterford Crystal factory. Anna flipped out at the display of all the elaborate items of cut crystal. As for me, I prefer a simpler, more rustic style, but I was impressed by the craftsmanship of the men who blew and shaped each object with incredible precision. It was fascinating to follow the whole process from a blob of hot glass to the perfect finished piece of crystal ware. And I was amazed at how many steps the work took.

Our second stage led us along the Irish south coast to the west, where we made a first stop at the seaport of Cobh. A local guide took us on a short tour, telling us all about the emigration from Ireland to America around the turn of the twentieth century. There were statues, monuments, and a huge palm tree to be inspected and photographed. Some of our group had their eyes more on the viewer of the camera than on the actual objects of interest. What I kept in mind was the story of fifteen-year-old Annie Moore, who was the first immigrant to enter the USA via Ellis Island on the January 1 1892.

"Here you see her statue with her two brothers, looking at the homeland she is leaving behind. In

Ellis Island they put up another statue in her honour, but there she is on her own, looking forward to where she is going, towards the American mainland."

Then there was the *Titanic* memorial. Cobh had been the last port where the *Titanic* had moored before she set out in April 1912 for her fatal rendezvous with the iceberg. The last survivor of this terrible tragedy, a very old lady who had been a baby at the time of the catastrophe, had come back later to live in Cobh and had died just a short time ago. I didn't memorize her name, but I decided to look it up on the Internet back home.

Lunch break was at the Blarney Woollen Mills. A good guide knows that a good tourist doesn't live on culture alone but has more profane needs as well and likes to buy souvenirs. Visits to the toilets, feeding, and shopping had to be integrated into the schedule of a well-organized tour. To those who preferred sightseeing to eating and spending money, Niall recommended a visit to Blarney Castle. "Climb the steps to the top for fitness, bend backwards for flexibility, and kiss the Blarney Stone in that position for the Gift of the Gab. Which means you'll be a fast and smooth talker for the rest of your life," he said.

Then he announced that a professional photographer was waiting for us in the parking compound of the Woollen Mills and would take a group photo of us all. We were free to buy one or not; the photographer would bring the copies to our Killarney hotel in the evening. I didn't want my picture taken, but Anna persuaded me to line up with her in the last row. Niall joined the front row, where everybody was squatting or sitting. He went down on his left knee.

To my right I heard someone twitter, "Isn't he cute? Like a crouching Celtic tiger!" It was the Sunday school teacher from Wisconsin, the double-teeny with the yellow pony tail, whose girlish sounds had caught my ear more than once. Suddenly I was full of aggression against the unnatural colour of her hair and her chirpy voice. Apart from the fact that there was no such animal as a Celtic tiger! Maybe something like it had roamed around the Irish scenery just after the last ice age, but certainly not in a modern parking lot.

After the photo session, Anna and I preferred the shopping and lunch, Anna being too lazy and I too clumsy to climb all those stone steps in the castle, not to mention bending backwards. Anna bought a woollen jacket for her granddaughter with shamrocks stitched on the front. "Kitschy, I know," she said, "but I have to prove to that child that I have really been to Ireland."

I didn't buy anything. The clothes wouldn't fit me anyway. I had enough shawls, I didn't care for jewellery, and for all the other things I had no use. We were quite happy sitting outside under a big umbrella, the weather spoiling us with unusual warmth and undiminished sunshine. We had a view of the parking compound, which was filled with cars and coaches. Ours was visible at the back, squatting there like a short fat white caterpillar, the rear-view mirrors drooping down from its front like the antennae of a tired insect. Niall was leaning against the side of the coach, talking to one of his colleagues.

"He's looking at you," Anna said.

"Stop that nonsense!" Sometimes I liked her teasing, now it just annoyed me.

Suddenly I heard a slight crackling sound on my front and felt a tickle in the region of my breastbone. I looked down, but of course I couldn't see anything, as my upper body was covered up to my neck with a long-sleeved T-shirt.

"Will you come to the lavatory with me?" I asked Anna.

"Why? What's the matter? Are you feeling sick?"

"No, just something funny going on under my top."

There was a queue in front of the Ladies. Finally we could squeeze into one of the narrow stalls. Anna helped me to pull my T-shirt and undershirt over my head. She let out a low whistle between her teeth and whispered, "There are cracks!"

I could see for myself from above. A web of small fissures had spread all over the horn plate which covered my breast. I nearly fainted with surprise and excitement.

"Maybe it is possible after all to get rid of it," I whispered back.

With a strange feeling of elation I put my tops back on with Anna's help. It was time to go back to the coach. I walked towards it as if in a dream, beaming at Niall, who stood there counting his sheep as they arrived. What I didn't see was Anna winking at him behind my back, but even if I had seen it I wouldn't have cared. I began to believe that a miracle might happen. On the rest of the way to Killarney, where we were going to stay for the next two nights, I hardly looked at the beauty of the landscape. Also, Niall's lecture about traditional Irish music, underlined by a CD he played, were lost on me. I daydreamed, starry-eyed and with a beatific smile on my face.

That night I didn't skip dinner. On the contrary, I ate with gusto, falling into easy conversation with our neighbours at the dinner table. I even decided to go out after dinner. Niall had offered to take those of us who were interested on a short pub tour. So we set out through the streets and lanes of Killarney, ending up at the Arbutus, where a trio of elderly men played Irish traditional songs. One fiddle, one accordion, one guitar, and vocals by all three players. No electronics, no showing off, and no artificial virtuoso manners, just pure, honest traditional tunes. To my own surprise, I joined in with "Molly Malone". I had heard my mother sing it many times when she still lived; it had been her musical tribute to Patrick, her lost love. The song came naturally to me. My voice was lower than my mother's had been and was not trained, but Nelly always told me I was a natural, and sometimes she made me sing with her. But the older I got and the more our relationship deteriorated, the more I refused to sing. Now it was like my tribute to my lost mother, to join in with this most popular of all the Irish ballads.

Niall approached us with two pints of Guinness. "Wanna try?"

He sat down at our table without asking permission, as if we were old acquaintances.

Anna agreed to try the Guinness, but I refused. "Beer doesn't agree with me."

"Well, then I think I have something else for you, if you'll let me. Ever tried a good whisky?" he asked.

I shook my head. He went to the bar and came back with a shot of golden strong-smelling liquid in a heavy tumbler.

"Redbreast, twelve years," he said, holding the tumbler under my nose.

I nearly got tipsy just smelling it. Carefully I took a sip. First it burnt like fire in my throat. I coughed a little. Then a pleasant warmth started spreading through all of my upper body. And then it happened again—the slight crackle. I emptied the tumbler in one gulp and asked for a second one.

I'll never forget Niall's surprised grin and Anna's "Are you sure?"

"'Course she's sure!" said Niall, "The lady knows what's good for her!"

He got up to comply with my wish. I went a little easier on the second round, but soon I felt my head swim. Anna decided I had had enough.

"Your first time in an Irish pub, and you go at it like an old regular," she said. "Let's call it a night! You can practise again tomorrow."

Niall offered his help to see us home, but Anna refused. "We'll be fine, and you need a rest," she said to him. "Enjoy your pint!"

I woke up with a headache, but my mood was fine.

"Well, well!" Anna said, "Last night your first buzz, now your first hangover, and who do you have to thank for that?"

I groaned. "Mr Redbreast, I suppose. There's a first time for everything in life. Do you have an aspirin?"

Anna did. I washed it down with a glass of tap water.

"Anna, could you please take a look at my back? I think something's going on there, like on my front."

Anna lifted my nightshirt. "Cracks all over! Incredible! When did you feel it?"

"Last night around four. I had the strangest dream, which woke me up. Then I felt the cracking and the tickling like yesterday."

Anna was at least as excited as I was. "And what was the dream?"

"I've had it several times before, but never as vivid as last night. I'm sitting at the entrance to a large cave on a hill, looking out on a bay. There's thunder and lightning far away, approaching slowly with the wind. The wind speaks to me, hissing something like I should watch out for the time slot to find my deliverance."

Lux appeared before my eyes, looking a little dissolved around the edges. Whether that was due to my fuzzy eyesight or if he had tried the

Redbreast too, I couldn't tell, but I understood his message: "The dream is for real. Watch out for the time slot!"

As usual with Niall we took off "ahead of the posse", this morning to go around the Ring of Kerry. I had thought of staying in Killarney. The cracking of the shell put me in an emotional turmoil I didn't know how to handle. I felt like holing up in the hotel room.

Anna wouldn't hear of it. "Nonsense! You're coming! You need the distraction; otherwise you'll start brooding again."

So I installed myself in my seat, carefully arranging the cushion I always carried with me for comfortable seating. Anna made those cushions for me. I had several at home and a small version for the rare occasions when I went out. This small one I had been using on the tour so far, but somehow it felt inadequate now. With the carapace losing its rigidity, it also lost some of its stability. It became more difficult for me to find a comfortable sitting position. Finally I managed to install myself.

Much of the beautiful scenery that day, like the Gap of Dunloe, was lost on me. My eyes saw it, but I just couldn't take it in. As to Niall's flood of information, there wasn't much I kept in mind either. Some of it was about the country's fauna and flora. He explained that wolves and bears had been extinct long ago, but he didn't mention Celtic tigers.

What he did mention were snakes. "If they tell you there are no snakes in Ireland, don't believe them! After all, we do have politicians." Anna found that very funny.

The only thing that got me out of my preoccupation for a while was the Skelligs, a group of small islands on the tip of the Iveragh Peninsula. Monks used to live on the stony rocks of Skellig Michael, a small medieval monastery perched on a ridge, in small round stone houses that looked like igloos. The monks had nothing to live on other than the products of the tiny island. They grew herbs on the steep flanks and a few vegetables on the narrow terraces supported by stone barriers. There were fish, seabird's eggs, and maybe an occasional tough gull or albatross whose flying days were over. The monks lived on the island day in and day out, year in and year out, in every season and for centuries.

I felt like flying over to the ridge and moving into one of huts. There my shell could break away from my body. The stone igloo would give me cover. The mostly rough sea would prevent boats from setting over and mooring on the small pier. Nobody would mount the many stony steps hewn into the steepness by the hard labour of the monks. It would be the perfect place away from the bustle of the world, away from people's curious glances and their pity and their disgust at the sight of me.

Even from the distance where I stood, I could see tiny specks of light dancing on the huts. They were some of Lux's fellow glow worms. I could feel him connecting with them. Lux made me understand that the Skellig was not for me, that my freedom lay somewhere else.

Back in Killarney some horse carts were waiting to take us to Ross Castle. Anna wanted to go, but I retired to the hotel room to collect my thoughts and emotions. Anna came back after two hours, full of enthusiasm about the ride and the beauty of Ross Castle and Lough Leane in the National Park. Anna loved horses and had immediately made friends with Paddy, the piebald gelding who had drawn the cart, and Freddy the coachman, a real ruddy Irishman.

"He has three horses," Anna said, "working each in turns, one day pulling the cart, two days on the pasture. He seems to love them and care well for them."

I was interested, thinking of the brown mare of my childhood days in Idylliken, and suddenly sobs shook me. Anna barely managed to calm me down. Afterwards I was furious with myself.

"This roller coaster has to stop!" I said to Anna. "I'm going crazy!"

"Let's go to dinner. You'll feel better with something in your stomach."

Niall wasn't around that evening. Why did I even notice?

Day five came. On the program were the Flying Boats Museum in Foynes, the Cliffs of Moher, the Burren karst, and a night in Galway. In Foynes the weather was rotten. The flying boats, on the other hand, proved to be a highly interesting presentation about an aviatic episode in the first half of the twentieth century; they were an airline between the Old and the New World, with the airplanes starting and landing on water. A passage over the Atlantic cost a fortune and was affordable only for the super-rich. The Irish Hollywood icon Maureen O'Hara and her pilot husband Charlie Blair, a star in his own right, were involved. He flew the last scheduled flight from Foynes to New York in 1945, before the water airline was given up, being replaced by Shannon International Airport, with planes taking off and landing on the ground. Foynes also boasts the invention of Irish coffee, brewed for the first time in 1942 to warm up freezing passengers.

The whims of the Irish weather took a turn for the better. The Cliffs of Moher greeted us with the brightest sunshine. For me it was almost too hot, I preferred to enjoy the breath-taking view from the café in the visitor's centre while Anna took a walk along the Cliffs. The path was lined by stone walls to prevent visitors from venturing too close to the abyss. Niall didn't believe in stone walls, as he had declared before our arrival. He was all for taking responsibility for your own actions.

"Those who are foolish enough to go too close and fall off a cliff have nobody but themselves to blame," he said. "Security is a bit overregulated nowadays."

When we reached the massif of the Burren, my first glimpse of the wild stony landscape gave me a start. There are cave systems on the Burren, limestone slabs and a vegetation which reminded me very much of the Swiss Alps. The scenery and the view of the Bay of Galway resembled the pictures in my recurring dream. Was it possible that I would find my cave here—the magic cave which could be the key to my deliverance? Before we got to Galway, I decided not to go on with the tour. I wanted to stay close to the Burren. Lux agreed with me. Anna was disappointed.

"I was looking forward to the Giant's Causeway and Derry," she said.

"Another time, I promise. If I could do without you, I would. You know that."

"You're fine," Anna said in an attempt to use idiomatic Irish-English. "We'll see with Niall if he can book us a few more nights at the hotel."

"I don't want to stay at the hotel. I would prefer something smaller with less people around. I feel too exposed in a big hotel if we're staying longer."

The hotel, a luxurious establishment, was indeed big. It had a beautiful view of the bay, but it lay on the wrong side of it for my taste and intuition. We talked to Niall, telling him that we wouldn't go on with the tour because I felt uncomfortable and was coming down with something.

"Pity," he said, "but of course I'll do what I can to make you feel comfortable. If you don't want to stay at the hotel, I might have a solution for you. A friend of mine owes a B&B in Salthill, a little bit outside Galway, also with a bay view. I can put you up there and make him give you special service. He owes me one. I'll finish the tour and come back to see how yer doin' in two days."

"You don't have to do that," I said.

"But I want to."

"Why?"

"Because I have a feeling that I can help. End of discussion. It lies on my way home anyway. I'll be back. Let me call François to see if he has any vacancies."

François did have vacancies. Niall gave him explicit instructions on how to give us special attention, including lunch and dinner, which François normally didn't offer.

"Thank you," I said. "I'm sorry to be such a bother. May I ask you one more question?"

"Sure!"

"If I feel better soon, I'd like to go back to the Burren to visit the caves before we fly back home next week. What would be the best way to get to the caves?"

"That, young lady, is a fortunate coincidence. I suggest my private car. I live in Kinvara at the foot of the Burren. We passed through it on our way here; it takes about forty-five minutes to drive from Galway, depending on the traffic. I can take you to the caves; some of them are a short way from Kinvara."

Lux blinked yellow.

"I don't want to impose myself on you."

"You're not imposing, I'm offering. Now go to dinner, I have to check my e-mails and make a few phone calls."

In the morning we took a taxi from the hotel up to the Cashelmara estate, which indeed had a beautiful view on a lagoon, kind of a little bay in the big bay. François received us with a bustle of activity, carrying our suitcases and offering all kinds of information about his establishment and how he was running it. I noticed his foreign accent and Mediterranean good looks; he was definitely not an Irishman.

"I'm from Marseille," he said, "but this has become home. Originally I had planned on staying here for three years, five at the most, and sell the place at a profit. And now we have the crisis, and I wouldn't get more than a third of what I had counted on. Never mind. At least this place makes money, I'm always well booked."

He went on about his former career as a karate champion, his overhead cost, booking policy, what we'd get for breakfast, and how to turn the shower on. Then he showed us to our room, brought us a tray with tea and biscuits, and reminded us to call if we needed anything.

"Alone at last!" Anna said when he had left. "He beats any mother hen!"

"I think he's sweet," I said, "and obviously well instructed by Niall."

So we settled down at François's Bayview for the next two days. François made a fuss over us that we soon began to enjoy. He offered me a free foot massage when I said my feet hurt. For Anna he played Chopin on his shiny black baby grand piano, which was a little bit out of tune.

"Because you're Polish and Chopin was Polish, too. Chopin is my favourite."

François was indeed a man of many talents; among other things, he was a shrewd businessman who ran his establishment very efficiently.

Niall came back as promised after he had released his human cargo in Dublin. Lux turned the yellow on again. I became all alert and nervous. I sensed that something decisive was at hand.

"Can I talk to you alone for a minute?" he asked me soon after the exchange of greetings.

"Why? Anna and I have no secrets."

"Emily, I'm going down to the lounge," Anna cut in. "I think you should talk to him on your own. You're a big girl. I'll be within calling distance and can fend off François in case he wants to bring you another cup of tea or massage your feet again."

So Niall and I faced each other, sitting on the two upholstered chairs with the tiny round table in between.

"Emily, tell me what's really wrong with you!"

I went stiff. "What do you mean? I was exhausted like I told you and coming down with the flu."

"I don't believe one word of it!"

"What do you care? How dare you put the screws on me? You're overstepping!"

"I know, but I'm doing it for a reason. I have a feeling I know what your real problem is and that I can help."

I grabbed the handles of my chair, trying to push myself up to go to the door and call for Anna. Panic seized me. Lux flew in front of my face, blinding me with the strongest light he had to offer, and my knees went weak. I fell back into the chair.

"Please, Emily, I mean no harm. Hear me out! Let me show you something. Maybe then you'll understand."

Niall stood up and opened his shirt. On the left side of his naked breast, half hidden under the dark fur of his chest hair, was a huge horseshoe-shaped scar, ragged and with red welts.

Niall spoke slowly and in a low voice. "I had a shell on my breast for many years. It's gone. I was able to get rid of it. It is possible to get rid of a thing like this!"

He closed the buttons of his shirt and sat down again.

All my defences broke down, I put my hand to my mouth and bit the knuckle of my index finger, incredulous and shaking at what I had just seen and heard. Niall watched me. His smoky grey eyes tried to catch mine with a mixed message of understanding and sympathy. He finally hypnotized me into calming down. I took my hand away from my mouth and stared at the marks my teeth had left on the knuckle.

"Emily, are you ready to talk? Do you want to tell me your story, or do you want to hear mine first?"

I let out a deep breath and pulled up the blanket which lay on my knees. He helped me to put it over my shoulders.

"Tell me your story!" I whispered.

He did.

Niall's Tale

My story is not pretty. There are quite a few things I'm not proud of, but you need to know it all if you want to understand. I won't hold anything back, at the risk of shocking you. If something gets too much for you to stomach, just tell me, and I'll give you a break.

I grew up in the village of Kinvara with my grandmother, my father's mother. My mother died when I was less than two years old, I have no conscious memory of her. All I had throughout my infancy and youth was a sense of loss I couldn't define. I fell into dark moods from time to time, not speaking and refusing to eat. That's what I do remember. Also, I often had tantrums when I got out of the black hole, feeling a terrible anger against the whole world. Grandma did her best to deal with my moods. Her method was to spoil me rotten. Not the best strategy, I'd say when I look back now, but she was trying to compensate for my misfortune. She did it all alone. My grandpa had died long ago.

My father was no help. For a long time he didn't get over my mother's death either. And he didn't live with us; he lived in Galway, where he worked as a civil servant. He was a decent enough fellow, very introvert and correct, seemingly cold on the outside. He dealt with his grief by turning off his emotions. Sometimes I wonder if he is a turtle too. Many years later I understood that looking at me reminded him of my mother. So he reduced his relationship with me to a weekly visit, asking about my health, if I had been good, how things went in school, and so on. He never touched me, never cuddled with me or put me to bed at night, saying prayers and sweet dreams. Sometimes when he left after his visit, I was allowed to see him to the next street corner. Those were the most precious moments for me, when I had him to myself for a few minutes. I longed for his love as much as I missed my mother's. A few times I tried to put my hand in his. He usually pulled it away after seconds.

As to my needs like clothing, food, pocket money, and school, he was as generous as his position allowed. He was more reserved when it came to extras. Even his birthday gifts were always of the "sensible" or "useful" kind. Grandma overcompensated by secretly buying me anything my heart desired if she could half afford it. She also overcompensated on the affection, showering me with kisses all the time and making me sit on her lap at every possible occasion, until I began to refuse when I was around about nine years of age. I could tell I hurt her feelings, but that couldn't be helped. I set the boundaries, and she had to comply. As soon as I realized that I had succeeded in rejecting her endearments, I became a real bastard. I enjoyed the power I had over her, saying no whenever it suited me. I punished her for loving me too much. I punished her for not being my mother, though at the time I didn't understand the psychology of it and neither did she. She never told my father, protecting me even when I violated every rule in the book.

It became really bad after the episode with the bike. I was twelve at the time. My marks in school were mediocre. The teachers always told me I could do much better, that I had a sharp, quick mind and should show more ambition. I was a real minimalist, cheating often instead of learning. On the other hand I picked up things so fast that I usually managed to bluff my way through critical situations.

One day my class teacher spoke to my father instead of Grandma, suggesting he do something to motivate me; it was a pity that I didn't live up to my full potential. Father took it to heart. He promised me a bicycle if I'd be at the head of my class after the next term. The incentive worked. I really went at it, did all I could to catch up, and studied instead of cheating and copying. In no time I had the teachers pleased with me, pointing me out as a shining example of a pupil reforming his ways and getting ahead. This didn't make me exactly popular with some of my peers, namely those who had profited from me when they helped me cheat. I paid in money and sweets and sometimes in dirty magazines I pinched from piles of waste paper. There were a few fights with some of the guys after my reformation, but I didn't mind, I had a goal. Subconsciously, as I know now, it wasn't just the bicycle; I hoped even more for my father's love and attention.

I got to the top of my class, but not quite. At the end of the term one guy was ahead of me by a half point. I was second best. My father stuck to his word—I didn't get the bicycle. It killed something in me. One night I went into a hot rage and ran through the streets demolishing all the bicycles I found on my way. I didn't get caught. I sneaked back into the house at three in the morning. Grandma sat at the kitchen table sobbing. I felt sorry for her, but I wasn't able to tell her so. "I'm home and going to bed," was all I said. It was the last moment for a long time that I felt any emotional stir at all.

I slept through the next morning, missing school. Grandma didn't wake me. She called the school to say I was sick. When I woke up around noon it was there, small but unmistakable—the shell. I had always had a hard spot on the left side of my chest between the breastbone and the left nipple. I thought nothing of it; it was just there, not bothering me. On this fatal morning it gave me physical pain. It had grown overnight, a round shield under my skin, putting pressure on my heart, cutting off the rage but also all other emotion.

I became calm and cold. The physical pain stopped eventually. My body adapted to the new organ. Sometimes I ran my fingers over the hardness, feeling the structure of the thing under my skin. It reminded me of a turtle's shell. From the outside it was hardly visible, hidden by skin and my growing chest hair. I stopped getting into fights with the boys, because I didn't want anyone to discover the thing over my heart. A fist landing on it might have betrayed its existence. Avoiding brawls earned me the reputation of a coward. I just had to live with it.

When I turned fourteen, my father remarried. For a short moment something like hope arose in me, in spite of the compression of the shell. Maybe he'd want me to live with him now. Maybe his bride would like to have me, and we could be a family. She was a colleague from work, as he explained to Grandma and me. The day he brought her home to the cottage, I knew at once I had fooled myself. The woman had a narrow face and thin lips, and her manner was polite and cool like polished granite. Grandma and I went to the wedding, a small and short affair. We didn't even go to dinner, just had a beer in the pub next to the church. I drank my first Guinness, snatching the pint from my father before he could react, and then walked out. It was my way of telling him to go to hell. I refused all contact with him afterwards, much to Grandma's chagrin. He went on paying for me until I finished school, but I never saw him again. After his wedding, he stopped coming to the cottage anyway.

In the years to come the thing in my chest grew slowly. The cold reasoning that had taken over after the loss of my normal feelings had one advantage. It made me think of my future. What chances did I have? What did I want to do with my life? A good school record was important. I didn't want to get stuck in a queue in front of the dole office. Also, I didn't want to get stuck in some office like my father. I wanted as little commitment as possible in the field of personal relations and as much moving around as possible. So I got a job as a bus driver, which suited me just fine. I left Grandma's cottage in Kinvara to live in Galway, hardly keeping any contact with her. When I think back now what a cold bastard I was, it gives me the shivers.

In my free time I kept very much to myself, reading a lot. Sometimes I went out for a beer and music in the pubs of Galway. Music was the only thing which stirred up something like emotion in me, especially our Irish traditional songs. One evening as I stood in Tig Coili, there was a fat guy with a pint in his hand, acting boisterous and giving all the ladies the come-on. He wore a grungy black T-shirt, and his head was shaved; his huge biceps was covered with wild tattoos. I took care to stay out of his way, judging him as someone who was looking for a brawl. The band took a break, and suddenly he started to sing. It wasn't a wild or gaudy tune as you would expect from an appearance like his. He chose one of the most beautiful, melancholy ballads I know, the "Rich Man's Garden". The chorus goes:

> You lived in a rich man's garden,
> Fairest flower of all that grew
> In a world I had no part of,
> Where no harm could fall on you,
> And I never got to know you,
> For you never looked my way.
> So I left you in that garden,
> And I sadly walked away.

Everybody immediately went quiet after the first notes. His voice was fantastic, husky and mellow at the same time; it went right under your skin. It even found a way to creep under my shell, swelling up my heart until it hurt. Tears ran down my face without me noticing.

When he finished singing, I realized a girl next to me was holding a Kleenex to my face. I took it and blew my nose, discreetly wiping my eyes and cheeks at the same time. She asked me if I was fine, and I said yes. I don't remember much of what followed, only that I overdid it with the Guinness. I woke up in the morning next to the girl. It was my first time with a woman, apart from some clumsy fumbling with the sister of a schoolmate behind a hedge some years earlier. When the girl told me I had been amazing, I skipped her offer for breakfast and fled. How could I have been amazing, when I didn't even remember what we had done? I did remember though that I had been crying in the pub, and I hated her for having gotten to me in just that moment. From then on I avoided Tig Coili.

What I didn't avoid was women in the years to come.

***

Niall stopped talking and looked at me with a question in his eyes. I read his meaning.

"Go on," I said. "Sexual relationships and their complexities are no mystery to me. I can read, watch TV, and surf on the Internet. Second-hand information if you want, but you won't shock me."

So he went on.

***

The experience with the girl, whose name I never knew, did leave a mark on me, even if I couldn't remember the sexual act. It made me curious about what I could do to women, what it would be like to sleep with a woman, consciously next time, if you please. I was over twenty, after all, and some of my schoolmates had started sexual relationships at sixteen or earlier, bragging about it and calling the girls they had slept with chicks or sluts or even worse. Mostly they treated the subject as if it was a sport. Though I wasn't exactly a romantic, as you can guess from what I told you earlier, this kind of attitude disgusted me. It had more to do with the aesthetic side of the matter. I knew the girls they did it with, and none of them pleased my eyes. Of course I knew about the details of the act itself, and somehow it just didn't appeal to me. It doesn't mean I was free of sexual impulses. My hormones worked fine. I had my share of nightly erections, if you'll excuse my being frank about it. You said I wouldn't shock you.

So the next time I set out to have a pint, I did it with a strategy in mind, picking my target with cold calculation. I looked for someone pretty, with freshly washed hair and without pimples. Not too innocent, but not slutty either. I was careful with the Guinness and successful with the fishing. That's how I began to think of it—going fishing. I did a lot of fishing in the years to come. But I'm getting ahead of myself.

Anyway, I did get the girl interested in me. I even recall her name; it was Sheila. This time I took her home with me and went at it consciously and methodically. I was amazed at her reaction. She had obviously fallen for me at first sight, and she was all emotional about what we did. To her it was making love. To me it was just sex. I was so detached that I didn't even come, only later under the shower, when I finished with my hand what had started in the bedroom. I have no idea if she noticed.

With the excuse that I had to get a lot of sleep because I had to start work early in the morning, I made her leave practically right after the act. She was all understanding and empathic about it, asking me, "Please call me, darling, or shall I call you tomorrow? It was wonderful and I can't wait to see you again."

I didn't call her, and I didn't take her calls. Of course, it was inevitable that I bumped into her one evening. Galway is not exactly a big city, and the pubs are well concentrated in the centre. I gave her a BS story of how I was absorbed with my job and my grandmother's illness and was not in the mood for bonding right now, and I'd call her as soon as I could see the light at the end of the tunnel. She wanted to believe me, I could see that. Her eyes were full of tears and her manner full of bravado. As for me, I just felt cold, enjoying the power I had over her, being able to manipulate her emotions, and I despised her.

Many years later in a session with my shrink, I began to understand that it was really myself that

I despised. I saw myself as an object of interest, but not of love, because if I was worthy of love, my mother wouldn't have died, and my father would have given me the bicycle. My grandma doted on me just because she liked showing me off. If anyone like Sheila got hooked on me, it could only mean that she was stupid and didn't understand that I couldn't deal with all this whiny "Darlin', what's wrong with you? Is it something I said or did? I just wanna understand. Please talk to me." For me there was nothing to talk about. I just wanted to enjoy my power over women. It became an addiction.

Things went on like this repetitively for quite a few years. I earned myself the reputation of an unscrupulous womanizer, which was entirely justified. There was no joy in it for me, not even real satisfaction. It was just a habit, a calculated power play. The women who were clever enough to see through me kept out of my way, sometimes warning others—which often didn't help. Sometimes even a woman who could see my coldness would take me on as a challenge, trying to find out what was wrong with me and trying to be my saviour and teach me love to make me hers. It never worked. I didn't let the women come too close in the physical sense either, always choosing positions where they couldn't touch my breast and find out about the hardness under my skin.

Today I can't understand how I could have gone on like this for so many years. The time is just a blur to me, year in and year out the same routine, not really feeling, not really living.

I did do something with my brain though, a lot of reading and studying, subscribing to online-courses in various fields. Literature and history were my favourites. One day I saw an ad; National Tours were looking for tour guide trainees. I immediately realized that this would be a chance for me to get ahead, to get to a more challenging level of what I was doing. It meant dealing more closely with people; social competence was required. I decided I could live with that. It would just be a matter of polishing my manners and correcting my brogue to a more or less neutral English accent that would be understandable to tourists from abroad. The knowledge of Irish history and culture I already had; in my own unemotional way I was a patriot. I applied and was accepted.

The training was tough and lasted eighteen months. It had to be done on the side, in addition to your regular work. Not all trainees made it. I did. As much as I was capable of emotion, I felt moved when I received the badge during the graduation ceremony. It gave me some sort of pride. I'll never forget my first tour, with a supervisor watching my back. He didn't even make me nervous. I felt very confident and very much in control. It was the control I had been practising enough in the past years on all those women.

Of course female tourists were off limits. Professional distance had to be kept. Bantering and joking was allowed—anything to make the customers feel good about themselves and the trip. The trips made me feel good too, in the way of ego trips. I enjoyed showing off the knowledge I had gained, the joking and playing with words, soon knowing exactly which cue would get which reaction from the crew sitting behind me. I was able to string them along while driving, and with my back turned on them. Single women on the tours were scarce anyway. Usually it was couples, mainly elderly ones from the United States and Australia with enough time and money on their hands to go on the quest for their Irish roots. It was important to play on that. I began enjoying myself, and I even went easier on the women in my free time.

Then about three years ago, the near catastrophe happened that almost cost me my job and my freedom. Something got to me in a most unexpected way, and I lost the control which was so precious to me.

I was between two tours, going out in Galway and, after many years, for the first time to Tig Coili again. And you wouldn't believe it. There was the guy with the husky voice who had sung the "Rich Man's Garden" so beautifully long ago. This time it was "Isle of Hope, Isle of Tears" he started on. And then it happened. A completely pissed fool went at him, shouting "Shuddup" and pushing him against the bar. I reacted without thinking and attacked the attacker in a cold fury, letting my fists fly, until some people held me down to stop me from killing him. My punch was formidable, because all the suitcases I had lifted from the bottom of the coach on the tours had made me pretty muscular. I would have killed him. Never in my life had I experienced such a loss of control.

There my victim was, lying on the floor in his own blood, his nose shattered and one of his eyes rapidly swelling shut. Also, he had hit his head when falling and was obviously unconscious. The ambulance came and the police came, and before I had fully processed the enormity of what I had done, I was sitting in a cell. I'll skip the legal details of the trial that followed. I was lucky enough to find a half-competent lawyer who got me out on bail, convincing the judge that I hadn't meant such harm, having just been on the brink of burnout because of a difficult tour. Anyway, I was a first offender without any record of getting into brawls.

My record of hurting women didn't count.

I got off with a few months on probation and social service. The parole officer I had to report to considered me an unusual case. His customers were usually much younger, he said; a first offender my age was something special. I was thirty-nine. He was a shrewd fellow with an instinct for people. I felt really uncomfortable under his scrutiny, as if I was an open book to him. I hated that. Generally, others were an open book to me, but this time the control was not on my side. He sensed that this made me furious.

"Well, well, well," he said. "What are we going to do with you? What would be the best remedy in your case?"

I thought that was a funny way of putting it. I was an offender, not sick. Or was I? Of course I was, as I was soon to find out, because a second stipulation in my case was a few counselling sessions with a shrink—dealing with your anger, getting in touch with your real emotions. And so on. I thought that was really ironic: me, with my history as a paragon of control and lack of emotion.

Then I was amazed at the task the probation officer put me up to. "I'll send you to Sister Mercy's cat shelter. Ninety hours will do. Mercy and the cats will do a good job on you. And you'd better do a good job on the cats."

To this day I'm grateful to the guy. It was Sister Mercy and the cats who brought about the change in me. Without them I wouldn't be standing before you now.

***

It had grown dark outside. Niall lit the lamp standing next to his chair.

"Emily, is it getting too much for you, or are you up to hearing the rest of the story?"

"You might as well finish. I can't live with this cliff-hanger."

A smile lit up his face, and I realized that I was feeling very much at ease with him now, in spite of what he had told me. My professional mind cut in. Maybe it would make a good book one day, with his permission.

***

It turned out Sister Mercy was a nun, who had defected long ago from a Benedictine convent. She was a real character—and still is! She still manages her cat shelter and a few rogues on the side. Maybe one day you'll meet her, if you want to. She's a tough old bird, a chain-smoker, which is not so good for her complexion or her cough either. When I went for my first assignment with her, she welcomed me with a cigarette in the corner of her mouth, wearing an old nun's habit cut off at the knees over faded jeans. Her hair was cut short and stood in all directions the wind blew. She gave off a nicotine perfume. It was all over her and inside her house, along with a whiff of cat's piss. One of the cats was allowed to live in her home and was not entirely housebroken. The other cats she kept in groups in four huge cages—twenty-six animals at the time. Some had been living with her for years; others she could give away to new homes, especially the pretty young ones. Most of the cats were brought to her sick, half-starved, or injured, by people who had picked them up somewhere. She had her little enterprise well organized, lived on donations, and had special deals with two vets who came to look after the animals at regular intervals or in cases of emergency.

Sometimes she had to take cats to the vet's practice to be operated on, and that would be one of my duties, driving her and the cats to the vet in my car. The other duties would be cleaning the cages and the cat litter boxes and preparing and distributing the food, seeing to it that the cats that needed a special diet or medication got what they needed.

All this Mercy explained to me over a cup of tea when I first came. I had no experience with cats whatsoever. I didn't even like the animals—too furry, too unpredictable, purring one moment and clawing your hand in the next without any preliminary warning.

"The first thing ye have to do is make friends with Tripod," said Mercy. "That's the initial test. If Tripod accepts ye, ye can work here. Otherwise they'll have to find ye another assignment."

Well, I wasn't eager to go back to the probation guy. I didn't like the piercing looks he gave me. So I did my best to suck up to Tripod.

"Just let him come on his own," Mercy said. "That's lesson number one with cats. Ye have to let them come to you. No manipulating and ordering them around like ye can do with dogs. Cats only do as they please. And if maybe one day they do ye the honour of following yer call, they do it because they love ye, not because of obedience. So sit still and make contact with Tripod."

Tripod was called Tripod because he had only three legs. He was born with three legs, probably the result of extreme inbreeding in a horde of cats living half-wild on a farm. Mercy's Border collie Patch, a bitch with a white patch around her left eye, had brought Tripod home as a small kitten from one of her forays. She adopted the scraggly half-starved creature at once, developing a pseudo pregnancy and feeding the kitten with her milk. Patch and Tripod had been inseparable ever since. Tripod slept in Patch's basket, developed a sound self-confidence when he grew up, and took over the command of Mercy's household. All visitors, four- or two-legged, had to be approved by Tripod. Patch, the dog, was friendly once Mercy let you into the house, but she was a good watchdog, barking and snarling, when you approached the house without Mercy telling her it was okay.

So I sat there, letting Patch sniff my hand. She graciously accepted a pat on her head and then lay down at Mercy's feet. Tripod sat on the windowsill watching me suspiciously, swishing his tail from one side to the other. He was the ugliest cat I've ever seen. Apart from having only three legs, he was short-legged like a dachshund. He was of indefinable colour and pattern, something like grey-brown stripes combined with sandy patches, and his eyes were big and round and protruding, not cat's eyes at all. He looked more like a deformed owl than a cat. I tried eye contact with him. As soon as I stared him directly in the eyes, he laid his ears back and hissed.

Mercy grinned. "Typical beginner's mistake. Cats interpret direct eye contact as a threat. Look away and try telepathy."

Now that was a new one to me. I knew I could read people pretty well; I had to in my job. But telepathy? So I tried, saying in my mind, "Nice kitty. Good kitty. Tripod is a nice guy, and we'll get along just fine." I felt utterly ridiculous, but you wouldn't believe it—it worked! Tripod stopped swishing his tail, jumped from the windowsill after a few minutes, circled the kitchen table about three times, and finally came to sniff my shoe. I bent down slowly, reaching for his nose with my index finger. He took a sniff at that too. Then he gave my leg a short rub with his head and walked away to lie down next to Patch.

Mercy was pleased. "Well, me boy, ye've passed. Welcome to my home and the cat's paradise. Ye'll do fine. And now tell me why yer here. The probator hasn't told me much."

I felt really embarrassed having to tell Mercy why I had been sentenced. To go ballistic because of a song and a drunken fool. How pathetic is that for a guy my age?

She looked at me, dragging at her cigarette, and said, "But that's not the whole story, is it?"

"What do you mean? Am I supposed to give further explanations? I've come here to do my job. I'm willing to keep my side of the bargain. What more do you want?"

"Nothing. It's not about what I want. I don't want anything except the work yer supposed to do. But ye can't fool me. There's something really off with ye. Yer all tense and overcontrolled. Are ye married?"

"No."

"Girlfriend?"

"No!"

"Ah! Strappin' feller like you, there must be some woman in yer life."

"My grandma."

"My eye! Living with yer grandma?"

"Not really."

"See her a lot?"

"No. What's this you're giving me? The third degree?"

"Just tryin' to figure yer out for yer own good. One day ye'll talk to me. They all do, sooner or later. And they leave with a lighter heart when the job is done."

The "lighter heart" gave me a stab just below my ribs. Was it possible she guessed something? I decided no, she couldn't, but I felt extremely uneasy all the same.

Soon I found an efficient routine with the cats. At first I was just doing my duty, but after the first week I discovered their personalities. I became more and more amazed at how their characters differed, like people's. I began observing them after having done the chores, how they interacted, how they acted with me, and I was really proud that some of them started to come to me for a caress or asking me to play with them with their body language and meowing. Soon I could read the cats like I read people. I memorized their names like I memorized those of the people on my tours. I didn't do the long tours at the time, just day tours so that I was able to go to the shelter in the evenings. National Tours had given me three months to be done with the social work. I was lucky they kept me on at all, but they knew I was good, and they hated to lose a good tour director after all the effort and money they had invested in my training.

The other stipulation—the shrink—made me much more nervous. You're supposed to talk to a shrink and tell him your life story, while lying on your back on the couch. That's what I knew about shrinks. Well, it wasn't that bad. The shrink didn't have a couch in his room, just a second upholstered chair and a glass of water on a small table next to the client's chair. Or should I say patient? Probably, because during the first session I found out I was a patient. Sick. Pretty screwed up.

Actually, I had known it all along. Over the past twenty years I had seen how different my life was from that of my colleagues. Friends I didn't have. They married, had children, spent holidays with their families, and showed around snapshots of the kids and the wife. I was invited to weddings occasionally, but I always found an excuse not to go. As to family life, I saw Grandma on her or my birthday and at Christmas. We didn't feel comfortable with each other, and I knew I was breaking her heart by being so distant. I couldn't help it.

I didn't know what to say to the shrink. He had the details of my offence. He looked at me silently for a few minutes while I fidgeted in my chair.

Then he said, "The real story is not here, is it? You're not a basically violent person, and with your job you can't be a guy who loses control easily. I have your official file and some unofficial information which I consider much more relevant. Your reputation as a ladies' man, it's quite impressive when you look at it from a statistical point of view. How many one night stands per month? Are you keeping a record?"

I felt extremely embarrassed. In spite of my coldness I knew that my behaviour pattern was beyond the standards of decency.

The shrink let it go and started with the routine. He asked after my father, my mother, where I grew up, had I liked it there, liked my school, liked growing up with Grandma, and so on. Just giving him the dry details made me realize what he could read from them. And he wasn't the kind who went all mellow and understanding on you with moist eyes about your misfortune. He went straight for the jugular.

"You're a sociopath, but for a reason," he said, "and not beyond redemption, I think. Ever talked to anyone about your issues?"

"What issues? I am what I am. No."

"Can't help it, can you?"

I didn't know what to say to that, I just stared at him.

He sighed. "Look, you're not an adolescent with an underdeveloped brain and raging hormones. I can't coach or coax you. I have a feeling you know pretty well what you're doing. What bothers me most is this detachment, the lack of personal relationships and family ties. You've shut off your feelings very efficiently. The question is, do you want to go on like that or do you want to change something? If you want change, I'll be at your disposal, even for more than the six sessions assigned to you. If you don't, there's nothing I can do for you. It would be a waste of your and my time. I see you're doing time with Sister Mercy. That's the best therapy I can think of. If it doesn't work, there are not many options left. That will be all for now. Just keep in mind what I said."

He let me go after no more than half an hour.

As it turned out, he was absolutely right. The cats and Mercy were the best therapists. When the cats started liking me and came to me for love, their purring crept right under my shell. It had a loosening effect. All those vibrations they gave off, some sounding like a small motor, others like the soft whirr of an insect, had their effect on the hardness in my breast.

There was Jack, the white and ginger rowdy who mobbed some of the smaller cats. When I scolded him, he gave me the innocent look and rubbed his head on my leg. He was the one with the built-in motor.

Then there was Badger, a dainty striped tom, very elegant and gentle, who liked sitting on my shoulder to look at the world from above.

And Minny with the long white fur and green eyes, a beauty and didn't she know it. She could lick her silky hair for hours and my hand with it while I stroked her.

Al Pacino had a slit ear from a fight. He was very shy and wouldn't let anyone touch him, except Mercy. But he would sit opposite me when I talked to him and start purring, closing his eyes, when I was patient enough.

And Dido, the fat white and grey female with the hanging belly. She liked to sit on my feet wherever I stood.

And Screechy, the cross-eyed Siamese with the nervous temperament and piercing voice.

And Fatty, the lazy black Persian who hardly ever left his bed.

And all the others.

Last but not least, Tripod really came to love me, jumping on my lap whenever I sat down in Mercy's kitchen for a cup of tea. Half way into my assignment I couldn't imagine my life without the cats any more. I still go to see them and help Mercy at least once a week.

Mercy didn't say much. She watched me with the cats, and I could say she was pleased—not just because I was efficient, but because I made the cats happy. And they me. I was beginning to feel again. It was as though she felt it too. She would look at me sometimes, and her eyes, still bright and piercing blue, would give me non-verbal messages. "Ye'll be fine," they seemed to say, "and I'll be with ye all the way." Sometimes she put her hand on my left shoulder, triggering a current of warmth that ran right across my chest, circling around the hardness and making it vibrate.

One night when I sat with her in the kitchen, she got a bottle of Paddy from the shelf and poured us both a sip. Not too much—I still had to drive home. I was feeling especially mellow that night. One of the cats was sick, and I had coaxed her to swallow her medicine. The whisky made me even mellower. It was then when I opened up and told Mercy about my shell—that I felt it was beginning to crack, to loosen itself from my ribcage and breastbone. She asked to see my naked chest, and I pulled off my sweatshirt. With her nicotine-stained fingers she softly drew a circle around the hardness, and I broke down.

I don't know how long I cried and sobbed, she standing next to me holding my head.

"Shhh, me boy, yer fine. Let it out. Ye need that now. This is between you and me and Tripod, and we won't tell."

When my eyes and throat were dried out, she gave me a glass of water and a wet rag to wipe my face. And then I talked. I told her everything I've just told you. When I had finished, I felt a crack in my chest and a sagging weight under the skin. The shell had broken loose and was just hanging there hurting, as if in a pouch. Without thinking, I opened the drawer where Mercy kept her cutlery and got out the sharpest knife. I cut into the skin of my breast, following the contours of the shell, before she realized what I was up to. Her first reaction was to stop me. Then she kept still, understanding that I had no choice. I cut out a flap of skin, folded it up, and took the hard thing out. It almost dropped from the wound by itself. I laid it on the kitchen table, staring at it for quite a while. Mercy got a clean rag and the whisky bottle, poured the whisky on the rag and held it to the wound. It burnt like hell, and the blood was streaming. When the wound was reasonably disinfected with the Paddy and the bleeding had stopped, Mercy gently closed the flap over the bare flesh of my pectoral muscles.

"Sew it on!" I said.

She got a needle and thread, soaking both in the whisky. Then she set to work. Her hands were a little shaky, but she did her best. The shell we washed and wrapped it in a plastic bag. We cleaned up the blood while Tripod watched us with his owl's eyes from the windowsill.

That night I slept on her sofa. She covered me with a clean sheet first and a blanket on top. Tripod crept up later and kept my feet warm all night.

From then on I became human, a person with feelings. I was not very well-balanced at first. For a few weeks it felt very insecure and vulnerable, not being used to walking around without the armour around my heart. I went to see the shrink and told him what had happened. He was speechless. Never had he heard of a thing like that in all the years of his practice. I showed him the wound, which had healed nicely.

"There's nothing left to say. You've made it. I wish you all the luck in the world," he said when I left him. And I swear to you there was a tiny tear in his eye.

The Magic Cave

Niall went silent for a while. I could see that telling me his tale had taken a toll on him. He was spent. There was pain in the lines of his face, and he kept his eyes shut. When he finally looked up and into my eyes, it really got to me. His pain and my pain were the same. He might have gotten rid of his shell, but not yet had he got rid of the misery he had lived in and dealt out to others for so many years. It still weighed on him. There was no need for words. From this moment on we both knew that our fates were connected, that we had to work through this together. I held out my hand to him, and he took it. Then and there he took my heart too.

There was a discreet knock on the door. Anna. I called her to come in. She looked from me to Niall and back and saw at once that something decisive had happened.

"Tea?" she asked.

"Yes, please!"

She went down again to get the tea.

"Come stay with me in my house in Kinvara," Niall said. "I have a few days before my next tour. Kinvara is a small village with less than 1,200 residents, but it is a beautiful place on the Bay. It's a good starting point for excursions into the Burren. I can show you the caves you want to see, and we'll be able to find a way to deal with your problem. I want to do this. I want to help. But I have a feeling you will help me too. You're a strong woman, even if you don't know it yet. You will challenge me, and I need that. So, you see, I'm not just being altruistic. It's going to be give and take for both of us; we need the exercise in this. We need to find out how to live a life worth living, not just functioning. Will you come?"

"Let me sleep on it," I said. "Is it okay for you when I give you my answer in the morning? I have to talk to Anna."

"Of course. I'll be back."

Anna came back with the tea. We drank it together, not talking much. Before Niall left, he took my hand and held it to his lips, and I felt another crack opening in my breastplate.

When Niall came back in the morning, I had sorted things out with Anna. She absolutely wanted to fly back home as scheduled. Her granddaughter had her birthday, and Anna had promised to be there.

Anna was all for my staying with Niall. "Do it! I think you need that now," she said. "You need time to talk to him. He's still waiting for your story. Obviously he hasn't held anything back about himself. Now you should be equally open. And after all, you'll have the caves close by that you want to see so desperately."

So Niall made sure that Anna wouldn't miss the bus to Dublin Airport. Then he carried my luggage to his car and helped me into the passenger seat. How I hated to be so clumsy! Being helped by Anna I was used to, but with Niall I felt embarrassed.

On the road to Kinvara, Niall told me what had happened after his "redemption", as he called it.

Again I was amazed at his ability to talk and drive at the same time. I had already observed this on the tour with him. On the coach it was his duty as a well-trained and experienced professional, but in his private car it was different. These were very private and highly emotional issues he was talking about, and still he never gave me the feeling that he was distracted or not fully concentrated on the road. I felt safe with him.

He had gone back to the shrink who helped him to find a new balance.

"It wasn't so much that he was the shrink. It was his common sense and no-bullshit attitude I liked," Niall said. "After a few good heart-to-hearts, just sensible exchanges between two adults who knew what they were talking about, I felt ashamed and was ready to try out a new behaviour, to make up for my old sins if possible. Of course I couldn't go to all the women I had used and discarded; I didn't remember most of them anyway. But I did go to my grandma and begged for her forgiveness. She was overjoyed, and we developed a new relationship which did us both a world of good. It was high time too, because she had already gotten her death sentence. She had cancer; the doctor gave her a few months. We made the most of it. When she died I was able to be there for her. I still miss her very much. I even called my dad, but I wasn't able to face him in person yet. I have to do that eventually. At the funeral I stayed out of his way. He can't help being what he is. We'll have to find a way to forgive each other. Maybe I can even forgive his hag of a wife. She must have her reasons for being what she is. Everybody has."

When Niall's grandma died, she left him the cottage in Kinvara. He moved into it, doing a little repair here and some renovation there, but he hadn't got very far with it.

"It's not exactly a castle, but it's comfortable enough. The fireplace doesn't work; there must be something stuck in the chimney. So no cosy peat fire for you, but there's central heating. And your room is ready. I hope you like it. Nothing fancy. You're getting the view of Dungaire Castle and the Bay though, the opposite side from Galway. You can give François a wave from your window if you like."

We arrived in Kinvara around noon. The castle was there to greet us before we drove into the village. Though it is not inhabited by noblemen and fair ladies any more, it was restored in the twentieth century and is, prosaically, used for touristic purposes and as a filming location. It still presents an impressive sight. After I had admired it from my window, installed myself in my room, done the unpacking, and freshened up, we sat down to lunch. Niall had prepared a chowder, a salad, and cold snacks.

"I'm not much of a cook, I'm afraid. If you're really hungry we'll have to go to The Merriman. You can get a decent meal there."

"I'm fine," I said, "thank you. The chowder is just right for me."

"If you want, we can go to the Aillwee Cave later, as you're so interested in the caves. But I must warn you, it's very touristy, and it's also a Birds of Prey Centre, with masses visiting every day. There are other caves, less known and off the tourist trails."

"That sounds more what I'm looking for."

Over coffee I decided to tell him about my dream and why I was interested in caves. By then we were well into the afternoon. It was too late for long excursions. Also, I felt tired. Listening to him the day before and the hope he had raised in me to get rid of the shell had kept me awake at night until the early morning hours. I was excited and spent at the same time.

"I'd like some fresh air and a good cave," I said, "but not going too far. What would be the nearest cave from here?"

"A short drive into the Burren and a little uphill scrambling," he said. "The place is not spectacular, but again it has the bay view you like so much. It's a small shallow cave. Nobody ever goes there except maybe some young lovers who want a little privacy."

"Sounds just right. Let's go."

The uphill scrambling was a bit of a problem. There was no path, just knobbly grass patches and stones. I could only do it with Niall's help. The vegetation fascinated me; it reminded me very much of some places in the Bernese Oberland back in Switzerland. I used to spend holidays there with Nelly and Kurt when I could still walk normally, before the carapace had taken over most of my body. I always loved the area of the Saanenland, especially the Lake of Lauenen on top of Gstaad. Glendalough had reminded me a little bit of the area around the Lake of Lauenen, though the Lake was situated much higher, about 1600 metres above sea level. It was a place of magic beauty and peace, charging you up with a feeling of harmony, even with all the ramblers walking around. In Glendalough I had experienced a similar sensation of spiritual energy welling up and enveloping me.

The cave gave me a start. It wasn't big or deep, a limestone slab formed like a small protruding roof over its entrance. I knew at once this was the cave from my dream. I panted and nearly fainted. Niall noticed and helped me sit down at the mouth of the cave, where I tried to get my breathing under control.

"I'd like to be alone for a while," I whispered. "Would you mind?"

"If you're sure you're all right. You look ghastly pale."

He didn't like it, and I felt his concern.

"Please, just let me sit. I won't go anywhere."

"I'll take a walk, but I'll be back in half an hour at the latest."

I nodded and he went. I turned towards the cave and looked into the darkness. And there they were, the little spirits dancing, Lux among them. All my glow worms and many more, some of whom I had never seen before. They dragged long shiny trains behind them like little comets. They came closer, forming a web around me with their trains, going faster and faster until the web became a cocoon. It was a spacious cocoon, shimmering in all kinds of pastel shades like mother-of-pearl. I felt a warmth around me and a lightness in my heart I had never experienced before. Then the cocoon took on the shape of a huge egg, protecting me from the outside world and promising to hatch me into a new life. The spirits gathered around me in a circle. There were a few coloured ones, transparent pink and green, oddly shaped with pointed heads.

"Who are you?" I asked. "I've never seen the likes of you before."

"We are what uninformed humans call the leprechauns. They've made caricatures of us. But never mind; it can't touch or change what we really are."

"And what are leprechauns? Guardians, like Lux?"

"Not quite. We are challengers. Our mission is to activate and awaken the lazy and the dull, to get lives into motion when there is danger of stagnation. We lure and entice humans into action, promising them rewards for striving. Some of them are best put to action by materialistic incentives, so we bait them with riches. Some humans describe our efforts as hiding riches at the end of rainbows, because often they are not able to live up to their chances and make something of them. Their excuse is that you can never get to the end of the rainbow where the pot of gold is buried. But some get the message and succeed. They understand they have to scrape together and forge the gold themselves. And we don't mean just the gold in a materialistic sense.

Anything you make into a success is gold. Those who learn are elevated to a higher awareness. They become candidates for guidance."

"But who decides which humans are worthy of guidance?"

"The Spirit who is One and All. Eventually all humans become worthy of guidance and deliverance. It always takes many lives to live. There are old and new souls on Earth at the same time. But the Planet Earth is just a crumb, a passing moment in time."

"What am I? Where am I in my journey?"

"That is not for us to tell. Just go your way and do what you have to do. Take one step further in your present earthly existence. If you create happiness, you will get one tiny fraction of the way closer to the Eternal Spirit."

A knock shook the shell of the egg, and a voice penetrated its wall.

"Emily!"

A hand pushed through the shimmering fabric, touched my shoulder, and shook it.

"Don't touch me!"

Suddenly it was all gone—the magic egg and the spirits. My eyes took in the open landscape and Niall standing before me. He took his hand away from my shoulder.

"Sorry. Did I frighten you? You certainly frightened me. You didn't react to my calls for quite a while. You had such a faraway look on your face. Have you been sleeping?"

"Probably. I had the strangest dream."

He didn't quite believe it, I could sense that. Maybe I would tell him later what I had really seen. Would he take me for a fool or think I was crazy? I put off the decision for later. He pulled me up by my hands and helped me down the slope, and we drove back to the house.

After dinner we sat together in his living room. He got a bottle out from the sideboard and held it up, looking at me questioningly. I nodded.

He grinned.

"Thought you'd never ask," he said.

It was my favourite Redbreast. He poured us both a shot. After two sips I felt the pleasant warmth spreading in my body. I marvelled at the speed the big change in my life was coming about. If anyone had told me a week ago that in a few days I would sit in a near-stranger's home in a foreign land drinking whisky and exchanging intimate confessions, I would have declared him mad.

It was my time to talk now. I had taken my decision to do so.

I began with what I had experienced in the cave. "It was not a dream, it was more like a vision, and it felt so incredibly real."

Niall didn't even seem surprised. "The little people, no wonder! And it felt good to you, you say? Then it must be good. Don't worry. I'm not considering you crazy. I've heard of weirder things. And when you think this is *the* cave, that's fantastic! Whatever happens next, I'll be with you in it. It's not only part of my repentance. It's also because looking at you makes me feel like a real person, a complete person with a palpable heartbeat, if you know what I mean. Ever since my redemption, I've kept away from women. It hasn't been easy, I can tell you. It was like going cold turkey after years of an unhealthy addiction. But I felt I had to do it. Of course I felt tempted more than once, but there was no woman who really touched my heart or made me feel even what I feel for the cats, Mercy, and my grandma—a stirring of warmth in my breast, my heart going out to someone. When I look at you I have that."

I could see he felt a little embarrassed after this confession, and my heart went out to him.

I broke the spell by asking him, "Do you want to hear my story now?"

"I do."

Emily's Secrets

I started with my childhood, the happy early years in my village. Those came easy to me. I enjoyed talking. Later it became more difficult. I had to take a break from time to time, but it had to get out, now or never.

After Nelly's and Kurt's honeymoon, they came to pick me up from GrannyPa's. Though the three of us were prepared for the parting, it was unbearable. Nelly got impatient and was obviously offended.

"I'm your mother, darling, and we're not going to other end of the world. You'll see your grandparents regularly. We'll visit them, and they'll visit us in the city. You'll have a nice room to yourself in our new flat, nice new clothes and toys, and a nice new doll is waiting for you. We can play games in the evening. You may even watch TV. There are nice children's programs."

I didn't care for all those niceties—I wanted GrannyPa, the old house, the nooks and crannies, the bubbly cow and the transparent goats in the stable, the glow worms, the river with the precious stones, the open country, and sitting on the brown mare when Grandpa took me to the orchard. I wanted to go to the village school with my friends Margrit, Robi, and Vreni, not to some city school where I didn't know anyone. And I didn't like Nelly calling me "darling". I even preferred Grandpa's "little turtle" to that. But there was no way out. Kurt put my small suitcase in the boot of his car, and Nelly made me climb on the back seat. I cried the whole way to Basel.

The house I was going to live in with Nelly and Kurt was located in one of the middle class areas in Basel. We had a flat on the first floor, two bedrooms, bathroom, kitchen, and a big balcony on the back. There was no grass, no river, no fruit trees, just the street in front and a paved back yard. My room was nice enough. The clothes and the doll were there waiting for me, and Nelly gave me a bath in the huge old tub with the lion's feet. Nelly was shocked when she saw the spot on my back. She sent me to my room and called GrannyPa on the phone. Her voice sounded all excited and angry through the door. I listened, but I couldn't understand what she said—just bits like "doctor" and "how could you . . .". Later I was allowed to watch a goodnight story on the TV in my new pyjamas, but I didn't like the TV half as much as the fairy tales I read from the book with GrannyPa.

Nelly and Kurt went out of their way to be nice to me, trying to prove how much better I was off with them. As I see it now, they did their best, but it would never be good enough for me. They put me to bed that first night, said an evening prayer with me, and kissed me on the forehead. Then I lay in the dark in my brand-new fancy bed with the pink sheet and flowery duvet cover, longing for my cot with the starched white linen in GrannyPa's house. I cried myself into sleep.

In the morning the patch on my back itched madly, and I scratched myself bloody. It had grown overnight; I could feel it with my fingers. Nelly was shocked again when she noticed the blood on my pyjama top and my fingers and saw that the patch was bigger than the night before. It disturbed her more than it disturbed me. She nearly got hysterical about it and made an appointment with the family doctor for the same day.

The doctor said, hm hm, he had never seen anything like it. We should see a skin specialist, and he would refer us. The skin specialist proved to be as helpless as the family doctor, saying strange things like "conservative treatment" and "surgical procedure an option". He would do some research to see if there were "precedents". In any case, the top of the spine was a difficult spot to operate on; it would be best to do some tests first.

Thus began the first series of doctor's appointments Nelly dragged me to. After the family doctor and the dermatologist, there were the paediatrician, the orthopaedist, the neurologist, the surgeon, and even a psychiatrist. The first series of tests were inconclusive. My blood levels were normal, and there was no sign of infection. The dermatologist suggested a biopsy of the hard material and took a sample off the surface. Under the microscope he could identify nothing but horn particles. Ultrasounds and X-rays showed a connection of the horn patch to the spine. It seemed to be attached to one of the thoracic vertebrae. The doctors asked me questions—had I always had the patch, when had it started, did it hurt, would I like to have it removed, and many more. I told none of them about the incident in the shopkeeper's back room. I just played dumb most of the time. After all, I didn't know myself why I wore this thing and no other child I knew did.

After I don't know how many doctor's appointments and me getting more and more moody and throwing tantrums at times, Kurt put an end to it. The doctors met for a council and didn't come to any agreement on how to treat my unique case. The paediatrician finally suggested waiting and seeing; maybe it was a juvenile condition and would grow out eventually. Nelly wasn't pleased at all. She wanted to consult more doctors, but Kurt stopped her. He made it clear that the whole thing was becoming an embarrassment to him, for even when doctors were sworn to professional discretion, there were always ways of things coming out in the open, and one of his most important clients had already asked him what was wrong with his daughter. Maybe Kurt could even see how much I suffered from all this fuss. Maybe it was one of the reasons why he made Nelly let it go.

So the first few weeks of living with my mother and her husband were dominated by all the excitement about my "disfigurement", as she called it. All the promises I had been given about the three of us becoming a happy little family went up in smoke. Whenever she spoke to GrannyPa, sooner or later the topic of my "disfigurement" would come up, and she accused them of not having taken proper care of me. I felt utterly miserable about all the fighting going on, about causing my mother so much trouble and not being perfect enough for her. For that was what it was all about. Nelly had this thing about perfection.

She herself was always perfect—perfectly dressed and coiffed, the make-up just right to accentuate her delicate features. She was lovely, with her green eyes, butterfly eyebrows, straight nose, and pointed chin which underlined the heart shape of her face. Only the mouth wasn't exactly to her liking, the lips a little thin, so that she did all kinds of tricks with various lipsticks to make them appear fuller. She was petite, with a girlish figure, and she looked younger than she was. Often people would take us for sisters. She loved that. I could tell that Kurt loved it too. It seemed to give him a kick when we went out together and people complimented him on his two lovely daughters. Not that he was old, just a few years older than Nelly, but his sedate manners gave him a fatherly touch. He insisted on adopting me. I was told to call him papa, which I never did.

Nelly had given up her job after the wedding in order to become the perfect housewife, mother, and hostess. She was meticulous about her fitness exercises, going to the gym twice a week. She took singing lessons to be perfect in the choir, always stressing that her solos were a responsibility that reflected on the choir's reputation. She wanted to be perfect with me, which meant that I had to be perfect to reflect on her perfection as a mother. There were times when I hardly dared to breathe without wondering if I did that perfectly enough.

Kurt and Nelly's strongest bond lay in the ambition they shared, the striving to ascend to the high society of the city, or what they considered as such. It meant the circles where the money and the power lay, the elite who pulled the strings either in the background or sometimes quite blatantly, making no secret of their leverage. Kurt was successful as a lawyer. Soon he employed a secretary and an assistant in his office and represented more and more VIP clients.

After only a year in the flat, we moved to a family home in one of the best residential areas of the city up on a hill. We had a garden with a small apple tree, flowers, a lawn, and a cosy patio behind some bushes. I was a little happier there than in the former place, where I had had to play with the other children in the street or in the paved backyard. I had hardly had time to make friends, but now there were new neighbours and new children to get acquainted with. We walked to school together. There was even a small cornfield on our way, the last cornfield on city grounds. We crossed it on a trail we made ourselves by trampling down the first small plants that grew in spring. The cornfield was abolished a few years later when the city replaced it with a road and a children's playground.

The school was nice, situated in a quiet green area. I liked walking to school. On spring mornings I could hear the birds singing in the trees before I entered the school building, and on sunny days their concerts came through the open windows into the classroom. I did well in school and even made a few friends. The patch on my back was no real problem yet. I followed gym lessons normally and was especially good at climbing and running. I got invited to some of the other children's homes and invited them back. Nelly was pleased because I picked the "right" children from the "right" families.

Nelly was happy to live finally in a "good" neighbourhood with educated people around. She made Kurt buy a piano, started taking lessons, and made me play too. Sometimes she insisted I sing with her, and she taught me a few songs. Some of them were Irish folksongs. She sang them only when Kurt wasn't home. So I grew up with "Molly Malone", "Danny Boy", "The Wild Rover", "The Connemara Cradle Song", and a few others. I could guess she was thinking of my father Patrick when she sang them. Those were the moments when I felt closest to her.

The two years from my eighth to my tenth birthday were more or less okay. I wasn't really happy. I still missed GrannyPa and my country home, but I felt all right. The visits to GrannyPa were difficult, because I cried every time when we left them. When they came to visit us in the city, I could tell they felt like they were on the wrong planet in our stylish home. The visits were alternated every two weeks. Nobody should be able to say that Nelly wasn't the perfect daughter either.

After I turned ten, things started changing. It was really nobody's fault; it was just me growing up. Before my body started showing signs of puberty, my mind grew up. One Sunday when we drove up to Idylliken for the usual visit to GrannyPa, I looked at things with different eyes. Suddenly the magic was gone from the old house; the nooks and crannies held no fascination any more. The glow worms on the spiral staircase seemed to be reluctant to show themselves. I could see only faint reflections. In the stable I was looking for the bubbly cow and the goats in vain. They had gone. My awareness was changing. It was part of leaving your childhood behind, as I know now.

Even GrannyPa looked different to me. I saw an old man with hard lines around the corners of his mouth and an old woman with bitterness in her eyes. I went out to look for my old friends Margrit, Vreni, and Robi and found them behind the school playing on the gym yard. They appeared like strangers too. I had nothing to say to them, and I soon left with a lame excuse. In the shed at the back of the house, the swing Grandpa had put up for me was still hanging in the door frame, but the swinging gave me no pleasure. Also, my legs had grown. I dragged my new shoes on the floor. Nelly wouldn't like the scratches on the polished leather at all. And when I had to use the outhouse, it disgusted me.

My old country home, the place of my former happiness, had ceased to be the haven I had always cherished. My feeling of belonging was gone. As I had never felt like I really belonged with Nelly and Kurt, I didn't belong anywhere now. I was utterly alone in this world. I was a changeling. When I kissed GrannyPa goodbye before going back to the city, it was like kissing two strangers. For the first time, I noticed a body odour on both of them which had never disturbed me before. It was the smell of people who had no bathroom to wash in.

On Monday morning the patch itched terribly. It had grown considerably overnight. Suddenly it formed a little hump and became visible under my clothes. Nelly had another fit of hysteria.

From then on things started deteriorating fast. The more Nelly made a fuss, the more the patch grew. I refused to see the doctors again. I screamed or locked myself in my room when Nelly tried to coax me into coming to a doctor's appointment with her. Still there was not much more than a small hump on my back, just a cosmetic problem. Again Kurt intervened, and tension grew between Kurt und Nelly. I could hear their heated discussions at night through the closed doors.

After four years of primary school, I entered grammar school, deciding at twelve to attend the branch that specialized in modern languages. English was my favourite. I picked it up with ease, though my French and Italian were not bad either.

The hump was more pronounced now, but I could still follow the gym lessons. One after the other the girls in my class got their periods. I was one of the last. The day I went home from school in the middle of the day because I had noticed the blood between my legs became a memorable occasion, but not in a positive sense. Perfect planner as she was, Nelly had already bought sanitary napkins and all the other stuff you need to manage your period. When Kurt came home in the evening she told him I had become a "woman". Kurt offered his congratulations and looked at me in a way I didn't like at all. It was just a short glance at my budding breasts, and Nelly didn't even notice. But suddenly he reminded me of the shopkeeper in Idylliken who had kissed me in the backroom. That night I started to lock the door of my bedroom.

Nelly kept telling me not lock myself in. She should always have access to my room in case something happened at night, a fire or an earthquake or some other emergency. I ignored her orders. It became a constant topic of discussion between her and me. Kurt kept out of it and just gave me one of his looks from time to time. One night when I lay awake after two in the morning, I noticed a barely audible noise at my door. I turned on a small flashlight which I kept in the drawer of my bedside table. The handle of my door moved downwards, but as I had locked it in spite of Nelly's reproaches, it stayed closed. I turned the bedside lamp on, knowing the light would be visible through a crack between the door and the door frame. The door handle slowly went up again. I kept the light on for the rest of the night.

From then on my trust in Kurt was gone. I showed him a cold shoulder whenever I could. A silent and subliminal war was going on between us. Nelly noticed, but she ascribed it to my "coming into puberty", telling Kurt I would come around eventually. I hated her for being so blind. Again there was a dark secret I could talk to nobody about. After all, nothing had happened. There was no proof the handle had been turned down by Kurt, and even if I could have proved it, there remained the question why he had tried to get into my room at night. He could have claimed he had heard me having a nightmare or something. But I knew what was on his mind, and he knew that I knew. Things became strained between us.

That was when my carapace really started to grow, at an incredible speed too. One morning a piece of horn broke through the skin on my breastbone. Within a few weeks it developed into a breastplate, and at the same time the patch on my back grew down over my waist. The breastplate stopped growing after it had reached over my navel and covered my pubis. From then on I became a person of non-interest to Kurt and a constant object of worry and embarrassment to Nelly.

She tried to drag me to doctors again. I refused, though I did agree to just one visit to the family doctor because I needed a certificate for school. Following gym lessons had become impossible for me.

The following years were uneventful. Nelly, Kurt, and I lived in the same household, but there was no warmth and not much communication between us. In school I had no real friends. I blocked any attempt of others to establish closer contact with me. I considered myself a freak, excluding the possibility that anyone could really like me. I did well in school though, and I passed my final exam at eighteen.

Nelly made one more attempt to make me see various doctors in order to do something about my "disfigurement". I even went along with it, thinking of my future and what options I would have in my life without the shell. There were the tests again, the various medical disciplines, the X-rays and the ultrasounds, and another interdisciplinary council. In particular, there was the new star surgeon, who obviously was dying to take me on as a unique challenge. I hated the guy at first sight—his egg-shaped head and deep-set eyes behind rimless glasses. He devised a plan to solve the problem surgically. Nelly, Kurt, and I were invited to the council, where he presented his strategy for removing the shell. He mentioned the risks, namely of possible damage to nerves and bone structures, not excluding a certain degree of paralysis. But what excited him most was the possibility of publishing my case in the *Lancet* and other renowned medical magazines. He even offered me free treatment if I gave my consent to comprehensive and complete publication of all the details of my condition and treatment. The other doctors seemed to be all for the plan; they would be involved in the publication. It would earn them fame in the international medical scene.

I ran, literally. I left the council before the star surgeon had finished his slide presentation, and

I never looked back. From then on I refused to even talk about medical treatment.

After my eighteenth birthday, Granny secretly gave me the papers to take control over the bank account she had kept for me. It was the money she had got for selling Fiona's house nearly twenty years ago. I was of age now and could do with it what I wanted. She also gave me my real father's birth certificate and the family photo of him, Paul, and Fiona. I hid everything in my room.

GrannyPa had become old and frail. Nelly wanted them to move to a residence for senior citizens, but they refused. The old house was their home. They'd rather die in it than enjoy more comfortable living arrangements somewhere else. The following winter Granny got pneumonia. GrannyPa played it down. When Nelly phoned, they just spoke of a cough and said that they had everything under control. Well, they hadn't. On our next visit to the village we were shocked at Granny's condition. Nelly immediately called an ambulance. Granny was taken to hospital, Grandpa going with her. They kept him in the hospital too; he had already caught the germs from Granny. Granny died on her second day in hospital, Grandpa three days later.

Their loss left me numb and inconsolable. They were the only two people who had given me their unconditional love, who had made me feel secure and good about myself, and whose love I had been able to return with all my heart, even if I had looked at them with different eyes since the time I turned ten and had seen them for what they really were with all their flaws and frustrations. The funeral service was held in the little church in Idylliken. It had been renovated in the meantime, showing off restored medieval frescos which had been discovered some years previously.

The church was more than full. Some people had to stand outside during the ceremony. GrannyPa had been respected in Idylliken; the old scandal about Nelly and Patrick was forgotten. The new sensation was my disfigured appearance. I could hear the whispering behind my back and see the stares I got from most people. The only highlight was meeting Mark, my uncle, who was only ten years older than I. He had become a sociologist, working on some scientific project. His parents, Grandpa's youngest sister Julie and her husband, couldn't come, as they were both immobilized by chronic diseases. Nelly was obviously happy to see Mark and introduced him to me. They had kept some contact over the years, but I had never met him.

Mark looked at me, and that was when I nearly lost my self-control. I had willed myself not to cry. The attention I got because of my appearance was already too much. Crying would have made me even more conspicuous. I immediately felt close to Mark; I saw an understanding in his eyes that was unexpected and consoling. He kept close to me during the whole ceremony and afterwards when we went to the funeral meal with the invited guests. I felt a quality in him that soothed some of my grief and unhappiness. We didn't talk much; his presence was enough. When he took his leave, he gave me his card and asked me to keep in touch. Nelly eyed this suspiciously. I had a feeling she was jealous of the attention Mark gave me. But she had to stick close to Kurt, who was playing his part as the grieving son-in-law perfectly.

What happened after the funeral was the death sentence for any chance I might have had to improve my relationship with Nelly and Kurt. There was the question of what to do with GrannyPa's house and the land. It was valuable property because of its location in the centre of the village, and the orchards on the sunny side of the valley would get a good price too. I immediately declared I would like to keep the house, renovate it, and go to live there. Nelly and Kurt looked at me with amazement.

"You just got out of school. You don't have a job and an income. How would you pay for all this, plus for your own livelihood?"

"I've inherited money from Fiona, my other grandmother."

There was a moment of silence. My parents had to digest that.

"How much?" Kurt asked.

I told him, and he smiled sarcastically. "That's peanuts," he said. "We'll get much more when we sell."

"But it's family inheritance. Doesn't that count for anything? I love that house, and you don't really need the money, do you?"

"That's not the point," said Kurt. "It would just be incredibly stupid to give away a property like that for such a ridiculous price, even to a family member. And how would you manage your life up there on your own? After all, you can't do without help in your condition."

Unfortunately he was right. I was physically handicapped, and running a household on my own would have been impossible. But it was the way he said it that made me hate him for the rest of his life. I understood that he was punishing me for not letting him get close to me, and I also understood that Nelly would side with him, not with me. I left the room with a nearly uncontrollable fury in my gut. I was close to going to the kitchen and getting the sharpest knife out of the drawer. From then on I was bent on punishing them both, thinking day and night about the best way for revenge. They did sell the house and the orchard, and Kurt even offered me a share of the profit with a sardonic smile on his face. I refused.

The chance for revenge came sooner than I had expected. One evening Nelly and Kurt prepared to go to the theatre for a ballet. They had a subscription for the first nights every season; it was part of their social status. In Nelly's favour I have to say that she honestly loved opera. The neighbour's daughter was supposed to go with them. She was thirteen and wanted to be a ballerina. I had caught Kurt more than once giving her the looks he had given me before I became a turtle. While Kurt was getting dressed in the bedroom, I watched Nelly applying her make-up in the bathroom. As I stood there, on an impulse I pulled out the dagger for a stab at her heart.

"That's nice of you to take little Viviane. Kurt will especially enjoy her company. Have you ever noticed the looks he gives her?"

Nelly went pale and stopped fiddling with her lipstick.

"How dare you!"

"You know it's true. You can't be that blind," I said coolly. I walked away and locked myself into my room, not reacting to Nelly's knocking and screaming. Kurt came running. They started an argument in front of my door. I held my hands over my ears.

From what I heard later they didn't take Viviane. Nelly called the neighbours with some excuse, telling them to call a taxi for the girl at her expense. Then Nelly and Kurt took off in the car. Kurt was driving, and probably the argument was still going on. But there was no question of missing the première. On the way into the town centre, a drunken driver crashed into them frontally, killing himself and both of them instantly.

***

I had to stop talking after that, breathing heavily and trying to hold back tears. Niall got up from his chair and bent down to me, trying to hold me.

"Please!" I pushed him away. "I hate to be touched! It has nothing to do with you. Just the hands is okay, but not my body."

He sat down again. I managed to look up and at his face. It showed so much understanding and compassion that I cried after all. He waited patiently until I was able to go on.

***

Though I had hated my parents, I felt terrible about the accident. It was my fault. I had caused the fight that certainly had distracted Kurt and disturbed his concentration while driving. Also, I was completely helpless. I had no idea how to deal with the practical side of this sudden death. Then I remembered Mark and called him. Without his help I probably would have jumped from a Rhine bridge, I was so desperate and stricken with guilt. Mark was my rock, not only in organising the funeral and all the legal issues concerning my parent's estate, but also in being there for me. I told him what had happened before the car crash and how guilty I felt.

He shook his head. "You shouldn't. The crash would have happened in any case."

"How do you know that?"

"My pendulum told me."

"You have a pendulum? You believe in this kind of superstition?"

"It's not superstition. The pendulum has never lied to me. But it's okay if you don't believe in it; most people don't. Maybe one day you will turn to the pendulum for help. All you have to do is ask. In the meantime you can rely on me whenever you need me."

Mark also helped me to sell the house and buy a smaller one on the other side of the city. My parents had left me a small fortune, since Kurt had done very well professionally. From Nelly's side there was also the money from the sale of GrannyPa's home. It had been bought by a neighbour from the village and pulled down. The neighbour built a block on the site, which he sold later at a good profit. The money I inherited from Kurt and Nelly came too late to save the beloved old home, but at least it gave me the means to live independently for a few years and time to think what to do with my life. My options for a professional career were limited by my physical condition. Also I hated to be around people.

There's one more thing I have to mention. When I was going through Kurt's desk to sort out his papers, I discovered a hidden compartment. It was filled with pornographic photos of very young girls, from eleven to fourteen years old guessing from their appearance. It didn't really come as a surprise to me, but I was still shocked. I could only imagine what it had cost him to keep his inclinations under control. I was sure he had never acted on them; it would have been too much of a risk. Probably the night when he had his hand on the handle of my bedroom door had been the only attempt. I burnt all the pictures in the fireplace. Nobody would ever know—except now you.

This was the time when the Internet began to conquer the world of communication. For me it was a blessing. I could hole up in my study and do everything over the Internet. There was the TV too, which brought the world to me instead of me going out into the world. Also, I read several daily newspapers and many books, preferably in English. I started studying all sorts of things by myself, my first priority being to perfect my English which had always been my favourite foreign language. I surfed on the Internet for hours, looking up whatever came to my mind. I watched TV compulsively, soaking up documentaries, news, and soaps as they came. I had help in the house on a daily basis. Apart from the string of women and some men who did chores for me, I had no contact with the outside world—except for Mark who visited me occasionally. Sometimes I ventured into the small garden and sat on the patio behind the tall bushes, hidden from the outside.

After three years on my own, I had gathered a huge amount of information about life and the world, all second hand from the media. And suddenly the idea hit me what I could do with my time and hyperactive brain. I started writing. I dipped into the huge pot of my virtual experience, making bits of it into a novel. On the Internet—where else?—I looked for a publisher and found one who was interested. He reviewed my manuscript and asked me to come and see him. I refused, explaining to him on the phone that I was disabled and couldn't go out. He insisted, and finally we reached a compromise; he would come to see me. He came, and I found him easy to talk to. His name was Thomas. He was a thin little man in his fifties, an old fox in the publishing business who knew how to make a profit.

"I won't beat around the bush," he said. "Your text has potential. Our house publishes two kinds of books, those which give us prestige and those which make money. Yours would be in the second category—easy reading for everybody, good entertainment, a little shallow but not too shallow. I'll give it a chance."

We came to an agreement on the contract. I insisted on a pen name. He would have preferred me to make public appearances for the launching of the book, but he understood why I didn't want to be seen in public. From then on I put out one book per year. They all sold pretty well, even if none became a bestseller. My income grew, and after five years I didn't have to worry any more about using up all my money.

Ten years ago I got fed up with all the temporary help in my home. Mark helped me to look for someone to live in, and we found Anna. She is a trained nurse, and I needed that. My physical condition deteriorated because I hardly moved or ate. Anna immediately agreed to live in. It saved her the trouble of finding a flat and paying rent. Also, I could feel that she liked me, and I felt I could trust her. We soon became close. Anna built me up, made me exercise my limbs a little, and created a special diet for me. She became my motherly friend and confidante.

In spite of Anna's good care, I started to slide into depressive moods after last Christmas. Don't ask me why, I don't know. It just happened. In May Mark insisted I had to do something about it, something drastic, or I would fade away.

"What do you suggest?" I asked him.

"You have to do something out of character for you. It must even be uncomfortable. Go out into the world and look at it first hand, not just second hand like you have done all these past years. It's the right time for you. You have the chance for a big change in your life, of overcoming old boundaries."

"Physical boundaries too?"

"It's possible."

"Is that what your pendulum says?"

Mark laughed. "It does. I can't fool you."

"And where do you suggest I go?"

"What do you think? There is one root of yours you haven't explored."

"Ireland? What does the pendulum say?"

Mark grinned and got the pendulum out of his briefcase. He held it in front of him with his eyes closed and concentrated for a few seconds.

"Ireland it is," he said.

The Storm

"The rest you know," I said to Niall. My mouth was dry from all the talking.

"Tea?" he asked.

"Yes, please."

After tea we went to bed. I slept through half the morning. When I got up, breakfast was waiting for me in the kitchen. Niall had already gone shopping and was busy repairing a window frame. We were both somewhat embarrassed, not knowing what to say to each other. So much had been said in the last two days. We were near-strangers who had spilled out all their secrets to each other, and this sudden intimacy took some getting used to. At the same time, I felt comfortable with him, and he with me. It was all very confusing.

Niall suggested going for a drive on the Burren in the afternoon. He would show me some places of interest like wedge graves and some beautiful views. I agreed. Often during the course of the afternoon he had to take my hand to help me over the difficult terrain, with the mix of soft grass and hard limestone. His grip developed a nervous intensity that began to make me nervous too. I had no experience with erotic tension, but I guessed it was a possibility from his side. It made me feel insecure. I had never had to deal with such situations. Since I became an adult woman, I had hardly ever encountered men, and certainly none had taken an erotic interest in me. I had no impulses of the kind whatsoever. The carapace had squashed them effectively from early puberty on.

At dinner Niall pushed away his half-filled plate. He looked at me with a longing in his eyes that made me extremely uncomfortable. As much as I was beginning to feel attached to him, I wasn't prepared for this kind of intensity.

"Emily . . ." he started, not knowing how to go on.

We faced each other over the kitchen table, both feeling utterly insecure in different ways. Abruptly he got up and pushed his chair back.

"Can I leave you alone for a while? I have to go to The Merriman. I promised the boys I would have a drink with them tonight. I won't be long."

"Go ahead."

He went and I felt relieved, at least for the time being. I did the dishes and then settled down in the lounge trying to read, but I found it difficult to concentrate. After an hour I decided to go to bed. Then I heard him come home. He opened the door to the lounge and stood in the doorway, swaying slightly. His eyes were bloodshot and his speech a little slurred.

"Emily," he said again, but this time he went on. "You know you've gotten to me, don't you? I'm going mad around you, not being able to touch you. I can't live like this. I don't give a damn about you carrying a shell. I wanna make love to you. If you can't give me your body, give me at least your lovely hands and mouth. I'm burning!"

I was shocked and felt utterly helpless, afraid he would come close and touch me. He didn't. Drunk as he was, he noticed the look of horror on my face, turned around, and staggered into his room, where he collapsed on the bed. Within seconds he passed out, lying there with his clothes on. I closed the door to his room and fled into mine, deciding I would move out in the morning. Then I cried myself to sleep.

That night I dreamt the dream again. It was more intense than ever before, really frightening, and it felt very real. I dreamt I was waking up in bed, sitting in my usual half propped-up position, because a storm was sneaking into the room through the crack of the slightly open window. The storm raged at the foot of my bed before the wall, appearing like a 3D-movie, though I wasn't wearing 3D-glasses. It came with dancing black clouds, bellowing thunder strokes, and crackling lightning that seemingly hurled themselves at me and pierced my eardrums like a Dolby surround sound system turned up to maximum volume. My impulse was to flee, but I was paralyzed and couldn't move a limb. At first I was terrified, but then I realized the din was turning into structured speech and was talking to me.

"Go to the cave. The time is right!" shouted the storm, repeating the words again and again, each time a little lower. Simultaneously the vivid 3D-rendition dimmed, until finally picture and sound faded away.

It was only then that I truly woke up, screaming at the top of my lungs. My screams roused Niall, who crashed into the room and turned on the light, swaying a little after his evening of intense carousing with the Lady Guinness. But he was obviously alert enough to have reacted within seconds to my screams. He did not present a pretty sight, with his tousled hair, crumpled day clothes, and stubbly cheeks, and the reek of the beer reached my bed before he did. Heavily he sat down on the side of the bed, staring at me from half-closed, bloodshot eyes.

"What's the matter?" he asked in a raspy voice, slurring the words a little.

I was so desperate that I grabbed his hand in spite of what had happened a few hours ago, and went from screaming to sobbing. I could tell that his impulse was to put his arm around me in a consoling gesture, but he knew better. So he waited patiently until I got the sobs under control.

"Nightmare?"

I nodded. When I found my speech again, I told him about the dream.

"Go back to sleep. It's over," he said, trying to push himself up to a standing position. I wouldn't let him and clung to his hand, still shivering. Suddenly I felt a hot current building up under me, creeping under my shell, picking up speed and running through my encased body up into my brain. It exploded there like a tiny rocket, shooting out stars from the root of my nose between my eyes, and in a split second I understood the time had come. Still holding Niall's hand, I pushed away the bedcovers and prepared to get up.

"What are you doing?"

"I have to go to the cave. Now!"

"Are you mad? In the middle of the night? And with this weather coming up?"

Only then did I notice that in fact a real storm was brewing outside. My mood turned to one of elation.

"But that's just it! Don't you see? This could be my deliverance! I can only find it in the cave! This is the time slot I have to use. It is tonight or never. I'll go. You can't hold me back! I'll call the taxi."

"For heaven's sake! Do you really think our Kinvara cabbie is waiting for your call at this hour? He'll be fast asleep with the phone switched to voice mail. Of all the possible time slots, do you have to choose the one when I'm in this rotten condition?"

"Did you have to get into this rotten condition?" My reproach came out sharper than I had intended.

He hung his head and shook it, ran his hand through his hair and over his prickly cheeks, rubbed his eyes, and let out a resigned sigh.

"I'll walk if I have to!" I shouted.

"Don't get all worked up. Of course I won't let you go by yourself. Just give me the time for a cold shower and a quick hot coffee. Then I'll be ready to drive."

A pang of conscience nearly made me refuse his offer, because he was not really in a condition to drive. As if he could read my mind, he said, "I've been worse and never lost control."

A quarter of an hour later we were on the road. Niall had changed into a track suit and rain jacket. The beer stench was reduced to a mere waft, and he was moving with his usual precision. I wondered at his amazing recovering abilities.

I was still shaken and slightly shivering. What added to my agitated state was an observation I had made while dressing hastily before we left. There was a crack running over the front side of my carapace, a median line from top to bottom which hadn't been there before. And it seemed to me there were vertical cracks on both sides too, from my armpits to the rim of the shield over my thighs.

Lux was with us in the car, right in front of me in the left corner of the windscreen. His shiny form was flickering and changing colours from light blue to pink to soft green and yellow. He did that only when something unusual was coming up. That was the reassurance I needed, that I was right about the time slot, the cave, and the decisive moment. What I was not sure about was whether things were going to change for the worse or the better. What role would Niall play, and how would it affect him? Was I putting myself in danger? Was I putting him in danger? I connected with Lux, who gave me to understand that he couldn't tell me or coach me. It would invalidate the chance I was about to seize.

"Are you talking to someone?"

Niall's question startled me. Was it possible that he sensed my contact with Lux? Lux's colour briefly turned to clear yellow, which suggested a yes. I could tell that Lux was happy about it, as far as a spirit free of earthly emotions can be happy. So let me say that he acknowledged Niall's new sensitivity, the channel he was obviously opening towards an extended awareness.

"I did," I said to Niall, "but I'll have to explain later. Time is running out, and we're nearly there."

It didn't take us more than ten minutes to reach the site of the cave. The moon was hanging round and bright above the karst scenery, casting shadows where the rocks protruded over the grass patches. I could see the cave from below, the huge slab which formed the roof over its entrance and the dark gaping mouth I was determined to walk into and let nobody stop me. What was waiting for me in this darkness? Niall turned off the motor and helped me out of the car. I felt clumsier than ever, and my knees were shaking, but there was no time to lose. The clouds of the approaching storm were closing in on the moon. I didn't mind the darkness. I had Lux to light the path as he had lighted the stairs for me in GrannyPa's house so long ago. But Niall was swearing.

"Goddammit, the flashlight is not working!"

"Forget the flashlight!" I said. "Just look ahead on the path. There will be a light you can follow!" I said it without thinking, taking it for granted that he would see Lux.

Niall gave me a puzzled look just before the moon was swallowed up by a mountain of clouds, but obviously he followed my advice. I heard him suck in his breath, but this was not the moment to linger and wonder. Lux beamed yellow and hovered upwards towards the cave. Niall's hand found mine, and suddenly there was no more need for talking and asking questions. Our minds connected like I had always connected with

Lux. There were three of us now. We scrambled up the steep hill as fast as we could, the shell compressing my lungs more than ever. Only Niall's grip on my hand kept me from falling. When we reached the cave the first lightning cracked, immediately followed by the roar of the thunder. The storm broke loose right on top of us. More lightning followed, lighting up the cave and dazzling our eyes. I got quick glimpses of the back wall of the cave, and I searched for the thing or the happening that would bring about the big change, that would deliver or destroy me. I wasn't afraid for myself any more, only for Niall. He sensed it and sent his answer to my mind, expressing his determination to be in this with me as he had promised. I saw Lux at the back of the cave, being his quiet soft white self again. I put the question to him what to do, but he kept still. I understood that it was all up to me now, and to Niall. We were on our own.

For a second I was on the brink of anxiety and desperation. Then I felt a slight cracking on my breastplate again, like the sound of crumbling when you break a hard biscuit in half. And suddenly I knew what to do. I ran outside into the gushes of the wind that were attacking the mountainside from the west, planted my legs firmly into the ground before the cave, and reached up with my arms to the black sky. My mind called the lightning. "Come and relieve me!"

"What are you doing? You'll get yourself killed!" Niall's mind and body rushed after me, trying to pull me back into the cave. What followed was a very fast exchange of thoughts and a physical struggle.

"Leave me! The lightning is going to break this hideous shell. Maybe I'll die in the process, but I have to take the risk. I can't go on like that, not being able to really live, to feel the sun and the wind and the water on my skin like I did when I was a child. And the touch of people who love me. Not being able to live as a woman, giving you the love you need. Not only the love in my heart, but that of my body, though I don't understand those cravings yet. I grew this damned shell before I began to understand about physical love. I want to desire you as you desire me in spite of my ugliness and disfigurement. I want to be free either way, alive or dead!"

I sensed a pain that cut right through my heart and realized it was Niall's pain crying out to me.

"Please, don't do this! Don't let yourself be killed! I know what I said a few hours ago in my drunken stupor. My bad old habits and my desire for you got the better of me. But please, I've come to my senses! I'd rather have you as you are, shell and all, because I can't imagine my life without you any more, even if I'll never be able to make love to you. I don't want to lose you! Just stay alive, for me and for yourself!"

Disregarding everything I had told him about how I didn't want him to touch my body, he threw his arms around me, joining his hands on the curve of my backplate. I sensed some more of the crumbling I had experienced earlier, and I felt the crack on my breastplate opening. The lightning struck at the same time, throwing us to the ground.

For a while we lay there, numb and not sure if we were still alive. The first thing I noticed after coming to my senses was an unpleasant smell of burning hair. But it wasn't hair that had been burnt; it was the surface of my backplate. It had cracked in several places. The pieces stuck to my skin, and there was the smell of blood too.

"Niall! Niall!"

He groaned and moved. He was dazed but unhurt, except for his hands, which showed a few burns where they had lain on my shield. I saw this in the shine of Lux, who had joined us right after the lightning had struck. Now the rain was pelting down, and the wind drove away the centre of the storm. We were safe. And saved.

The physical aching didn't matter. There was the pain of Niall's burnt hands and the pain in my whole body, which was a mess of broken shell and torn skin, from which the pieces of shell hung, pulling with their weight. I ripped my clothes off without wasting a thought on nakedness. In the past few weeks I had felt the carapace loosening in front and at the back. It was breaking away from my breastbone and my spine, until it weighed mainly on my shoulders. In some areas it had also detached itself from the epidermis. A new but very delicate and very white skin had already grown there, but in other places the shell was still attached, and blood was oozing from the broken skin where the pieces hung. I started pulling at the fragments my hands could reach, ignoring the pain and the blood. In a few seconds I had torn off the breastplate, which stuck only to a few small patches of skin over my ribs. And then I saw it for the first time—my breast. My two breasts, which until now had been covered and flattened under the plate, like the breasts of the poor Spanish infantas in Renaissance paintings, or those of Elizabeth I of England, a queen who had forced herself into decorative armour, not daring to be really a woman. They had also been smothered by breastplates, those of inhumanly tight gowns that squashed their womanhood before it could bloom.

The moon slipped out from behind the wandering clouds as I looked down on the front of my body. I had last seen it uncovered more than twenty years ago, an infanta myself then, before it had grown the ghastly bodice around my budding form. My fingers wandered over the landscape of bleeding wounds and tender white skin, exploring the alternate sensations of pain from the touch and pleasure from soft stroking. I cried.

"Don't hurt yourself!" Niall's voice sounded choked.

He startled me. For a moment I had forgotten he was there. I looked up in his face and saw tears running down his cheeks. His hands came up and towards me but stopped in mid-air. Anxiously he looked at me, remembering how I hated to be touched. Then our minds connected, and he knew I was not afraid any more. Still he hesitated, so I took his hands and put them on my breasts. For a moment they lay there and the world stood still. There are no words to describe what we felt then, the magic and the miracle that was happening to us, so I won't even try.

After a while practicality took over. There was still the shield on my back, pulling at my skin.

"Tear it off!" I called out to Niall.

He tried, and I cried out in pain, so he stopped.

"I can't tear your whole back off," he said, "and I can't bear to see you in such pain!"

"The pain is worse when I can't get rid of it," I replied. "Please, do it. Deliver me of this monstrosity no matter how it hurts! You did it to yourself. You cut your own breastplate out from under your skin because you couldn't bear it any more. So do this for me, please! I would do it myself if I could, but I can't reach far enough back."

Cut! He had cut himself free. That was it!

"Do you have your pocket knife with you?"

Niall reached into his pocket and got the knife out. Still he hesitated.

"I'm afraid of doing too much damage," he said.

"What about the damage we have lived with all our lives?" I said. "I'm not afraid. I trust you. You have experience with this. If I cry or groan, don't mind it. Just cut!"

I know I sounded fierce, but I couldn't help it. He folded up the largest blade of the knife, wiped it on the sleeve of his jacket, and started cutting. My cries were cries of pain and exhilaration at the same time, with every bit of shell that came off. Finally it was done. Blood was dripping from my back. I turned round to face Niall. He looked ghastly. His face was white and his eyes wide open with the horror of what he had done at my command. When he saw the joy and the relief in my face, his colour came back. He dropped the knife, let out a deep breath, and sat down heavily on the wet grass. I sat next to him, still naked, enjoying the pain of the wounds and the cold night air piercing my skin, as though they were precious gifts. I leaned towards him, and he very carefully put his arm around my shoulder. For the first time. We sat like this until I became aware of Lux dancing in front of us.

"You're right, we have to get back," my mind said to Lux.

"I suppose we do," said Niall.

"I wasn't talking to you," I replied softly.

He looked at me questioningly.

"Look!" I said.

Niall became aware of Lux again and of the connection of our minds—his own included.

"I'll be damned!" he whispered.

"No, you are not!" I said gently. "On the contrary. I take that as an expression of your astonishment, but please try not to use it any more. Let's go home."

"Home? You said 'home'! Until now it was always 'your house'."

There was nothing to comment on in that, and no more talking occurred until we got—home.

But before we left the site of the cave I had to get dressed. Fortunately, the rain had started again so that we could wash some of the drying blood from my body and from our hands. The blood wasn't flowing any more, but there were quite a few open wounds with ragged edges, and they hurt. There was blood on our clothes too, but the washing machine would take care of that. Gently Niall helped me into my dress, which looked grotesquely large and out of proportion on my now-thin frame. I didn't bother with my custom-made underwear; it wouldn't fit any more. And never again would. Never! I planned on burning all my clothes as soon as we got home. He would have to lend me some of his things, even though I would look ridiculous in them.

Before we scrambled down the slope to the car, I crept on the ground on all fours and carefully picked up the pieces of my shell that were strewn around. I wrapped them in my now useless undershirt to examine them later under full light. I wanted to study every detail of the terrible armour that had made my life so miserable for so long. I wanted to memorize the sight of the broken shell when it would be laid out before me, in order to understand what it was that I had carried with me and had finally cast off in such pain. Niall took the bundle from me and supported me on the way down to the car. I wasn't able to walk on my own.

At home Niall insisted on seeing to my wounds before we went to sleep.

"We can't risk an infection," he said. "The circumstances on that mountain were not exactly sterile, and my knife wasn't either."

Though we were both exhausted, he led me into the bathroom, where he got out disinfectant and all kinds of wound dressings. The disinfectant stung like hell, but it was a pain I welcomed because it would lead to healing. Holding onto the washbasin, I let him dress the tears, cuts, and holes in my skin as best as he could. I was barely able to stand upright. The loss of the carapace affected my balance. My body had been so used to carrying all that weight around. Also, my centre of gravity had rested in the big hump on my back, and now it had shifted to my lower body. My sense of balance could not yet deal with it.

Niall did a good job of dressing the wounds, as the mirror later showed me. With an elaborated system of criss-crossing strips, he had managed to cover up and close most of the wounds even though his own hands were painfully burnt. Then he pulled a clean T-shirt down over my head and gave me a pair of his briefs. To me this was the most wonderful outfit I had ever worn. Stumbling and clinging to his arm, I found the way to my bed. He pulled the covers over me, went to his room, and collapsed on the bed in all his clothes again, as he had done a few hours before. But this time for a good reason.

A New Dawn

I woke up to a sunset on the Bay of Galway. I had obviously been sleeping for the rest of the night and all of the following day. I heard Niall moving around in the house and noticed the smell of food. With difficulty I managed to push my aching body up to a sitting position, to turn sideways, and to put my feet on the ground. I didn't dare to stand up. I felt shaky and dizzy. As if I had given him a cue, Niall opened the door. His hands were bandaged, but he managed to carry a tray with juice, tea, scrambled eggs, and toast.

"Hungry?"

"Famished!"

He put the headpiece of the bed upright, made me lean on it, and watched me eat. Sometimes he had to help me. My movements were clumsy, and occasionally a tremble would run from my spine to my chest.

"It will pass," he said. "Your body has to adjust to its new condition. You will have to exercise it."

"In time, in time! I can't even stand upright or walk properly, let alone take up a fitness program!"

"One thing at a time. I have already devised a plan for building you up."

"Tomorrow! Let me go back to sleep. Right now, eating was enough of an effort."

I managed to pull his head towards me with one hand and kissed him on the cheek. A big smile lit up his face. Then he put the headpiece of the bed down, right to a horizontal position, not the half propped up one I was accustomed to. It felt odd to lie down—really lie, not lean. The memory of my childhood came back—my little bed behind the curtain in GrannyPa's bedroom and how I had stretched and wiggled in it to find my favourite sleeping position. Then it was my turn to smile. I smiled at the memory. The last thing I saw before closing my eyes again was Lux on Niall's shoulder putting his tiny translucent finger to his mouth and winking at me.

I slept all through the night and half into the morning. When I woke up, a chair stood next to my bed with some clothes on it—two dresses, a moss-green tracksuit, two T-shirts, two soft woollen sweaters, some underwear, and a bathrobe. I urgently had to go the bathroom and decided to do it on my own. Getting into the bathrobe I could do sitting on the bed. Then I got up on my two feet by holding onto the back of the chair. I managed to set one foot before the other, testing my new balance. I was leaning too far forward when walking, still instinctively trying to counterweigh the burden of the heavy shell on my back. Though my head knew the burden wasn't there any more, my body hadn't got the message yet. But it would, and the sooner the better! My determination carried me all the way along to the bathroom.

After using the toilet I got out of the robe. I stood slightly swaying in front of the mirror and looked at myself for a long time. There were two mirrors, the one behind the washbasin and a narrow high one on the wall to the left that reached down nearly to the floor. I stood before the tall mirror, taking in the picture of the thin figure looking at me and trying to define it as my own. It was difficult. The face I recognized, but not the body. The legs were the same as before. Two dents clearly showed on the upper thighs where there had been constant pressure from the shell. Between the dents up to the neck there was a form yet unknown. Much of it was plastered with wound dressings, some showing spots of blood that had seeped through. There was an amazing lot of intact skin though, amazing to me because the feel of my body indicated that it was one big aching wound. It wasn't so bad when I looked at it. The skin appeared very pale and thin, with bluish blood vessels and pink flesh showing through. I had already had a glimpse at my breasts in the moonlight two nights ago, but now I saw them in broad daylight and up front. It was a shock. They looked squashed, which they had been, of course, but it was still shocking to see how squashed. I knew what a normal female breast was supposed to look like. These two flattened globes, pinkish-white with the nipples pressed into the flesh, were a sight hard to bear. I swallowed a sob that rose up in my throat and willed myself to think positive, though it was an expression I hated!

"Think positive!"

Many times I had heard this commonplace from the mouths of people who didn't know what else to say to me, thinking it would cheer me up, pretending there would be a solution to my hump-backed condition—a drug, an operation, a miracle to make it go away. Even my ex-shrink had not been above such cheap advice. Well, the miracle had happened. What more did I want for the time being? I should be grateful and not get ahead of myself. Solve one problem at a time! You can't have it all and right away! It takes time! Time to realize that learning to live with a brand-new body may be unexpectedly difficult. Pull yourself together, and acknowledge how lucky you are!

I tried to turn from one side to the other to look over my shoulder at the back of my body. The attempt was not very successful. But one day it would be.

What I finally forced myself to look at was the dark triangle of my pubic hair. It made me shiver. At least this secondary sexual characteristic didn't look flattened. It was curly and thick, hiding well the sleeping beast hidden underneath. One day the beast would wake up and stir and demand its due, I was sure of that. It was what I longed for and dreaded most, the moment when I was truly going to be and feel like a woman. With Niall in the picture, that moment would come sooner or later. I felt very much afraid—afraid of trying his patience, afraid of not being able to meet his demands. Because I did want to meet them. My love for him filled my heart and soul, but not yet this poor ungainly body.

"Emily, are you in there?"

"Yes!"

Niall's voice and knock on the door made me reach for the bathrobe. He had seen me naked in the moonlight and afterwards when he dressed my wounds. I didn't care then because it had been an exceptional situation, but I did care now, and I wanted to spare him the sight of my ugliness. However, reason told me I couldn't spare him. My dressings had to be changed, and the alternative would be to have it done by a stranger, which would be even worse. Carefully, I slipped back into the robe, biting my teeth because the movements alone hurt like hell, not to speak of the pressure the robe put on some of the wounds, even if it was ever so slight. I decided to ignore it as best as I could.

Still not very sure on my feet, I opened the bathroom door. It took all my courage to look him in the face, fully awake now and very much aware of the new age which had dawned upon the two of us.

***

The weeks that followed were not easy. We had to find a new balance with each other, a way to deal with a kind of embarrassed shyness we had not known before. We were both afraid, because the real commitment was only just beginning, and we had no experience with it.

In desperate moments I turned to Lux. He kept very much in the background now, but I knew he would not leave me. He would be there when I needed him.

"Lux, what shall I do? I feel a burden to him and an embarrassment to myself!"

"Have faith in yourself. Have faith in him! You're ready to find your own way." Lux faded into the background, which was a sign that he thought I was doing all right on my own resources.

I resorted to being practical. So did Niall. We concentrated on organizing our life under the same roof, trying not to tread on each other's toes but to be there for each other. We were both loners, individualists, self-centred, scarred in every sense of the word. A lot of healing had to be done.

Priority number one in the first week after the Night of the Storm was the healing of my wounds and Niall's burnt hands. He knew a lot about medicine. He had to; it came with his job. If a medical emergency occurred on a tour, the guide had to be prepared. First-aid courses were obligatory in his training. I was medically quite well informed, too, but only through the Internet. With me it was all theory. I learnt from Niall. Soon I could bandage his hands better than he could. And he changed the dressings of my wounds every day, being meticulous about sterility. They healed astonishingly well, even the big ragged ones. Only once did Niall try to convince me to see a doctor, maybe even a plastic surgeon. The fierceness of my reaction took him by surprise. I told him about my experience with doctors back in Switzerland, how they wanted to publish about me, how they strove to present my unique condition to the world of science and get famous from it.

"What about your scar?" I asked him. "You didn't want to take your case to a doctor either, did you? You preferred cutting yourself free, and the result is not exactly pretty. Does it matter to you? You say no. Well, it doesn't matter to me either. If I don't like the look of my body, it won't be because of the scars that remain, it will be because I'm not familiar with this body yet and because my skin looks so unnatural and morbid."

I felt he was afraid of doing something wrong and causing me pain or an infection, of hurting my feelings by touching or not touching me, by looking or not looking at me, or by saying something wrong that would set me back in despair. I could tell he had never felt more self-conscious in his life. And neither had I.

After the first week things got better. Because of his hands, he had managed to postpone going back to work. The tour he had been scheduled for was done by a replacement.

"Aren't you afraid for your job? There must be a lot of competition around waiting for a chance to step in. Can you afford sick leave for such a trifle as a blister on your soft little paw?"

Niall grinned. We were back on track to playfulness and teasing.

"Don't worry. None can step in my big shoes, and National Tours know it. They're glad to have me, and they will be reluctant to let me go when I reach the age of a recycled teenager. But that's a long time to come."

We laughed. The embarrassment was dwindling.

The doctor he had to see for his medical certificate was a friend of his. Niall told him a sob story about how he had burnt his hands when trying to light a fire in the fireplace for a shivering lady, and that said lady had to stay on at his house to look after him now that he was disabled, and that certain injuries just took a long time to heal. He grinned when he told me. I could just about picture the scene between those two rogues and decided to use it in my next book.

"Old Rory is a sport. He gave me a certificate for three weeks. That's what I call a friend! Maybe one day you'll meet him."

"Maybe."

In the second week Niall decided it was time to get my skin used to daylight in order to build up pigmentation.

"You are a brunette, so you should have good pigmentation by nature, more than I do. Let's start with five minutes in the open air every day. Without clothes on, of course, and without the dressings. Not in full sunlight, and only after three p.m. And I promise not to look. That should be enough for starters. When your skin has become all thick and tanned to bronze, we can start with the power workouts."

"Don't get ahead of yourself! I won't enter any bodybuilding contest just now!"

We laughed, but I took his advice seriously and did as he told me. I was beginning to enjoy his bossing me around and devising plans for my rehabilitation. I stood in the garden stark naked every day, pivoting slowly like a chicken on the grill, counting the minutes on my watch, extending the treatment after a while to a minute longer per day until he called me back into the house impatiently.

"Don't overdo it!"

I checked the result in the mirror every night and was pleased with the change to my skin. It was still white, but it had lost its sickly pallor. The open wounds were turning into scars, and soon some of them would not need to be dressed any more. Secretly I massaged my breasts regularly with the oil Niall used to rub my back every day, a special formula from olive oil and herbs. The breast massages were my own idea, and I didn't tell him about them. My breasts were still a sore point to me, though I could detect certain small changes in their appearance. The nipples were not as flat any more, and their colour had gone from light pink to a salmon shade. I hoped that one day they would grow from the shape of fried eggs to rounded globes.

Soon the three weeks of his sick leave were over. Niall's hands looked fine. Still feeling fragile and unsure of myself, I dreaded the day when he would have to leave me alone to go on a tour. I tried to hide it, but by now we knew each other too well. He went to Rory again and came back with a medical certificate for lumbago, which would give us another two weeks. There was no need to ask him how he had persuaded the good doctor. Probably, he didn't even have to fake the lumbago, because by now old Rory had guessed there was something "special" going on in old Niall's private life. Niall kept the details of "special" to himself as he had promised me. One day he would enlighten his friend, but for now it was too early.

We settled into a household routine where Niall did the shopping and I managed things around the house as best as I could. It gave me pleasure to stoop to the washing machine and fill it with dirty stuff through the round door in its front. I had not been able to do that for mor than twenty years, with the carapace keeping me in a rigid position. I enjoyed picking something up from the floor without having to go down clumsily on my knees. I just bent down and took it. I carried all my turtle clothes to the back of the garden and made a nice pile of them, putting old newspapers and dry wood on top. I let Niall strike the match to light the fire. Later he drove into Galway to buy me some more clothes. He wanted me to come with him, but I still didn't feel up to it.

"You did all right last time," I said. "You matched my taste and my size too."

"You're lucky that I have a good eye for a woman's size," he mocked me.

"It's so good of you to remind me!" My voice sounded sharper than I had intended.

"Sorry!"

We left it at that.

In the third week I called Thomas, my publisher. He wasn't exactly pleased with me. My books made good money for him. Even though they were not really bestsellers, they sold steadily and had their fans. I had promised him a new manuscript after my return from Ireland, and that was overdue.

"Well, well! Do we have to slay a lamb for the prodigal daughter? Where have you been hiding? I called and I mailed and I even sent someone round to your place, but that housekeeper of yours pretended she had no idea of your whereabouts."

Faithful Anna. I felt immensely grateful to her. Of course she knew where I was. I had called her three days after the Night of the Storm and told her briefly what had happened, that she was to talk to no one about it, and that I needed time to recover. She was flabbergasted at what I told her, and she even cried a little, telling me how happy she was for me. She also promised I wouldn't be disturbed, neither by her nor by anyone else. She would wait for my call when I was ready.

I put Thomas off with a white lie—that I had gone to Ireland to get an operation that had been successful, that my hump-back was gone, and that sometime in the near future I would be ready to do all the stuff for him I had refused so far, like press interviews and TV appearances and readings and signing my books for readers. That mollified him. He agreed to wait until I presented myself at his office after my return, and of course he was thrilled that I had been able to do something about my "condition" and could now live happily ever after.

He definitely had read too many of my novels . . .

In the fourth and fifth week of my recovery Niall started me on a physical training program—exercises for balance, muscular toning, stretching, and even some yoga positions and dance steps. Niall proved more and more to be a man of many talents. It gave him joy to see that he could make a difference in my life, returning to me some of the dedication and understanding he had received from Sister Mercy. In a way we had both gone through purgatory, though we didn't really believe in purgatory in the biblical sense. But we agreed that there was some truth in the concept, purging through pain and coming out on the other side more mature and caring. It had happened to both of us.

My training program was successful enough that I felt reasonably strong and confident by the end of the fifth week. More important was the way Niall and I had grown together. Not entirely yet, but getting there. We would never be perfect, neither of us, and probably would still have occasional controversies and be angry at each other. But we had released within ourselves the ability to love and—equally important—to be loved! To let someone truly love you. Believing in being lovable and worthy of love. I had lost this belief after the loss of GrannyPa, but at least I was able to consciously remember this part of my childhood. For Niall it had been far more difficult. The loss of his mother had occurred at an age when a child has not yet built up a conscious memory. It was all the more remarkable, the long way he had come. He had developed all by himself the ability to love and care, with a little help from Sister Mercy and the cats, and he had achieved even to help me.

Finding Home

For me the time had come to face one more emotional challenge—the encounter with my other grandmother, Fiona from Inis Mór. The Internet had told us that Fiona still lived in her native village and had a small trade with homemade local products, in spite of her nearly eighty years of age.

When the day came, it wasn't one of the best to visit the Aran Islands. The sea was rough, and squalls of rain battered the boat. Niall held my hand during the whole rocky passage. We arrived around eleven in the morning. Close to the pier small buses were lined up, the drivers offering tours to Kilmurvy. There were pony traps waiting along with the buses. The animals fascinated me. The Aran pony is not big, but it is strong with an oval head, sometimes shaped like a Neolithic stone axe, and long thick fur growing down over its hooves. Obviously the fur had to be trimmed. Some of the ponies seemed to have entered a contest for the most stylish hoof-fringe. There was one huge horse with incredibly long legs, resembling a medieval war horse. It was tied to a bigger trap seating eight people. I marvelled at the strength of the animal.

"Let's take a trap to Kilmurvy. I'll keep you warm," said Niall.

So we did, wrapping a rough blanket around the two of us.

The village of Kilmurvy consists of a few scattered houses. We got off the trap and walked into the centre, a rectangular square lined by whitewashed cottages. One contained a café, while the others were tourist shops selling local products. "Wools, linen, jewellery" said the writing painted on the walls, big letters in Gaelic, smaller ones on English. There was also a visitor's centre with a presentation about the old fort of Dún Aonghasa, or Dun Aengus in English. This old fort was the main attraction of the island, about a kilometre uphill from the village. The centre was the starting point of the walking path to the fort, and no cars were allowed. Niall asked if I wanted to walk up.

"Later. I want to find my grandmother first."

We went into the first shop and asked. "Third one to the right," said the friendly woman, who was perched on a high stool behind the counter, knitting coloured woollen socks that she would probably add to the range of goods she sold. The population of the Arans live partly from their handmade products—pullovers, socks, caps, shawls, seaweed soaps, and other items—sold to tourists with certificates confirming their authenticity.

We went to the shop the woman had indicated. My heart was hammering against my chest. Niall took my hand and squeezed it and pushed me gently through the entrance. Inside stood an even smaller counter than in the other shop. The woman sitting behind it was also knitting and also seated on a high chair. She looked up when I entered, and her busy fingers came to an immediate stop. I looked into her eyes, clear and silvery as Granny had described them. Her formerly thick dark-red hair had gone old, white with a few coppery strands. Her skin spoke of the rough winds and frequent rains on the island, wrinkled but not dry. I could tell she saw Lux and the likeness to my mother in my face. She put her handiwork on the counter, climbed down from the stool, and came to me. Granny had described her as a tall strong woman. Now she was a waif, shrunk and a little bent, but still nimble on her feet. Her hands came up to my face and stayed on my cheeks. We both cried. I took her in my arms and held her for a long time. Niall kept in the background, fumbling with a Kleenex on his face.

Finally Fiona collected herself, looked up to me, and asked, "What is your name?"

"Emily."

"You are as beautiful as your mother, but softer. How is she?"

"She died, and my stepfather with her."

"I'm sad to hear that. So she did get married after all. Was she happy?"

I didn't know what to answer and felt embarrassed about it. "Sometimes, I suppose."

I felt ashamed. It dawned on me that I had never really thought about my mother's ability for happiness. It had probably been crushed very early when she lost my father, me, and her parents at the same time. When she got me back seven years later, the attempt to repair old damage didn't work. Replacing the need for happiness with ambition and the striving for perfection can never be more than a surrogate.

"Come to my home," Fiona said.

She looked at Niall and then at me.

"You are from the area," she said to him. To me she continued, "You are from here too. Your soul is, even if you were born and raised elsewhere. I can see it in the silvery flecks in your eyes."

She locked the door of her shop and put the "Closed" sign up. Her cottage was at a short distance on the outskirts of the village, with a small garden in the front.

"I grow the vegetables myself. The soil is very fertile. We use a mix of sand, seaweed, and manure on the island." The cottage was old and tiny, but well kept and freshly whitewashed. "I was able to buy it with what I make from my shop. My knitting is very much in demand with tourists. I learnt a lot from your Granny Frieda. I do stitches they don't usually use here."

She showed us proudly around on the inside. It contained three small rooms, the kitchen being integrated into the living room. There was a small bathroom with a shower. The furniture was simple, with no knick-knacks standing around. In a corner close to the fireplace she kept a small altar with a simple stylized Mother of God carved from wood. It wore no paint. Next to it stood a small wooden plate with a carving of the Celtic symbol for eternal life. These two icons of opposing religions, of the Catholic faith and the old Celtic ways, were obviously comfortable with each other.

Fiona lit a peat fire in the small fireplace for our sakes. The peat she reserved for special occasions, usually burning wood or coal. I had never smelt a peat fire before, and I loved it. We sat down to a cup of tea in front of the fireplace. There was a lot of catching up to do. I had the photo with me of her, my father Patrick, and my other grandfather Paul, and the copy of Patrick's birth certificate. With withered delicate fingers she stroked the documents.

"I remember the day when I gave them to your Granny. Frieda was a wonderful woman, the only friend I had in your village. I never felt at home there. When I came to Idylliken with Paul, I thought love would be enough to make you settle down and be happy. I was so wrong. I never belonged there. I always felt homesick for my island. But first there was Paul. I didn't want to leave, he needed me so much. After he died, it was Patrick I couldn't take away. I asked him if he would give the island a try. With all the horses on Inis Mór, he could very well have made a living here as a smithy, but he didn't want to leave. He desperately wanted to be accepted where he was. And he loved Nelly. He wanted to wait for her until she was of age and could go away with him. He believed in a future with her. He was heartbroken that Carl didn't accept him."

She sighed and was silent for a while.

"Your Grandpa was a good man, in his own stubborn way. He just didn't know how to listen to others. He was always convinced he was right and that it was his duty to be right and do everything his own way. Frieda was the only one who could stand up to him at times, but even she had been brought up in the belief that the man must always be right. She didn't challenge him as much as she could have. They both did love you very much."

"I know, and I loved them. We never got over the separation when my mother took me to the city to live with her. I did go back to visit, but it wasn't the same."

We talked a lot about my family. I opened up to her in a way I hadn't thought possible to someone I had never met before. She was so simple and so wise at the same time, with incredible insight into human nature. I felt I could tell her everything without holding back, about my shell and how I had finally succeeded in getting rid of it. Niall nodded at me encouragingly so that I knew I could tell Fiona about his shell too.

When we fell silent after hours of talking, the daylight outside had dimmed. Soon it would be time to catch the ferry. On the mantelpiece of the fireplace Lux was dancing, shining bright yellow, and he had a companion I hadn't noticed before.

Fiona smiled. "You see, I have my guardian like you, though I don't really need him any more. He came to see you and your spirit. They are two of a kind and part of the Cosmic Eternal Spirit who guides us all and knows no difference between religions and the artificial boundaries set by narrow-minded humans. Old ways or new ways, Celtic mystique or Christian belief, it's all the same to the Spirit."

She hugged me tightly and Niall too, looking from him to me and back.

"You are destined to be together," she said. "Not many lovers share the kind of experience you have. It is an unbreakable bond in the spiritual sense."

I felt embarrassed. "We are not lovers. We haven't . . ." I was at a loss of words, but Fiona understood.

"Even if you have not been to bed, you are still lovers. It's not the body alone which makes the love. The body only follows what's already there—sometimes sooner, sometimes later. Will you come back, Emily?"

"I will!"

We left her standing on the doorstep waving. The taxi was waiting to bring us to the ferry. We made it just in time.

Two days later Niall and I were sitting in front of the cottage in Kinvara enjoying the warm sun of early September. We didn't speak for a long time, but our minds were in sync. The scenery of the Bay of Galway would soon present us with one of its spectacular sunsets. The awkwardness had come upon us again, for we had to face the inevitable—parting after five weeks of incredible closeness. The intimacy had not been of the physical kind, which had been limited to helping each other with our injuries. It was the intimacy of discovering that someone was your soul mate, becoming a part of you, and the intimacy of healing together.

Lux blended in with the sun's rays as we sat on the bench; he was not needed for a while. In spite of the budding happiness Niall and I felt in each other's company, I could also sense a bitter note in his mood. He was a man, a passionate man, and the restraint he had put upon himself was taking its toll. Often I had heard him moan at night in his room through all the doors and walls, knowing what it meant—temporary and unsatisfactory release by his own hand. It gave me a bad conscience, because I still couldn't share his longing, I was content with the way things were between us, at least for the time being. But I was eager to get to know physical longing for his sake, to give him what he needed, and to share with him the melting of the bodies which meant so much to him and still nothing to me. So with all the closeness we enjoyed, there was this element of insecurity that made him edgy and me sad.

"Will you really come back?" he asked.

"I will. You know that!"

"I'm sure you want to, but what if you go back to your country looking as lovely as you do now? Mingling with the crowds like you never did before? What if you start enjoying attention from your fans when you show yourself in public, signing books in bookshops, doing readings, and being dragged around in the media? And what if you meet men who are keen on conquering a famous novelist?"

"Silly!" I said. "Nobody can hold a candle to you! You're one of a kind. You know that."

"Do I?"

"I've never seen you so modest."

I looked at his hands lying on his knees, those beautifully shaped hands with their incredibly long fingers. Some burn marks were still visible, but the skin had fully grown back. His fingernails were slightly spatulate and impeccably manicured in spite of the garden work we had been doing together the last few days. On an impulse I reached for his hand and took it into mine. His impulse was to pull me into his arms. It took all his willpower to refrain from it. Our eyes met, his grey melting into my green with incredible intensity. That had to do for the moment, and my heart ached for him.

We stayed on the bench until the sun had gone down and the evening chill came up. We went back into the house still holding hands. I could tell he was feeling somewhat reassured. He would drive me to Dublin Airport in the morning and then pick up a new group at two o'clock from one of the four-star hotels to rock them around the Island for a week.

"Amis and Aussies looking for their Irish roots," he groaned. "Well, that's the life I've chosen. But to be honest, I love my job. It's so much fun when you know how to make people feel good about themselves. I have learnt to do that, and now they make me feel good about myself too. What about you? You're going back to your job and your Swiss roots. Will you get stuck in Switzerland?"

"Darling, I've also grown roots here. You of all people should know. And my cousin Mark would say that in one of my former lives . . ."

"Oh yeah, give me a break with the former lives. I know all about them by now!" We both laughed, and the awkwardness was gone.

There was one more thing we had to do that evening. We drove up to the cave, carrying with us a bag with our shells inside. We had wrapped them in pieces of silk, his blue, mine green. His shell was small and in one piece, while mine was considerably larger and heavier and broken into many pieces. It was dusk when we arrived. We found the exact spot where the lightning had struck. The grass was still black and charred. Niall got a spade out of the trunk of his car and dug a hole. Lux helped with his shine when the daylight faded. Just when the hole was big enough, the moon came up. It was not quite full, but huge and of a bright apricot shade. We laid our shells to rest, covered them with earth, and heaped a good many big stones on top. By the time we had finished, the moon was smiling on us from above with a soft white light, similar to Lux'.

In front of the passport checkpoint in the departure hall of Dublin Airport we said farewell. Now that the moment had come, I was overwhelmed with the realization of how much I was going to miss him. My feet moved as though of their own will, taking a step towards him until our bodies touched. Slowly I lifted my arms and put them round his neck. For a fraction of a second he stood still. Then his arms came round me and locked behind my back. His mouth brushed my cheek and finally lingered on my mouth. I kept still. Then his lips parted and his tongue parted mine. He kissed me as tenderly as his mounting passion would allow. Theoretically, I knew all about tongue kissing and had never understood the thrill of it. Now I was beginning to. The emotional turmoil of saying goodbye cut a breach in my reserve. A new energy welled up from my insides, something like an electric current running from my body to Niall's and back. I had never known such a sweet sensation! Finally I understood.

I don't know how long we stood there kissing. We held up the queue in front of the passport check; people were walking around us, grinning. We didn't notice. Finally we broke away from each other, breathing heavily.

"Don't go!" His voice was hoarse.

I had to catch my breath before I was able to speak.

"I don't want to, my love, but I have to. I've made promises I must keep. I have to wrap up a few things at home and clear things up. There's Anna I have to take care of. She's taken care of me for so many years, and I want to help her find a new position. I want to say goodbye to GrannyPa and my parents just one more time. Maybe their spirits will show themselves to me when I go to their graves. I want to go to my real father's grave. I want to tell Mark he must come and visit us and not forget to bring his pendulum. And maybe I'll even look up my former doctors, if they are still around, to show them how a 'practically incurable condition' can be healed without their help, with a magic they know nothing about, because they are so fixated on repairing human machinery. And I'll tell them they may publish my case study now. I'd gladly give them all the information, knowing for sure they won't do it, because they would be declared insane by the scientific medical community."

He found his smile again. "Pretty mischievous! And then you'll come back?"

"Yes, my love. And to do away with the last of your doubts, I'll leave Lux with you. I can do without him for a while. You need him more right now."

He let me go then. I watched him walk away with a spring in his step and Lux on his shoulder. With a spring in my heart I moved on to the booth to present my passport.

***

On the airplane from Dublin to Basel I began sketching out my decisions. I had a lot to sort out. I would keep the house in Basel, letting Anna live there. She would look after it and keep it ready for me when I wanted to come back at times. We had already talked on the phone. As a professional nurse, she could easily get a job in a hospital or do day care in private homes.

Thomas, my publisher, was impatient to see me. I would go over my new manuscript with him and give him time to arrange the kind of marketing campaign he had always wanted me to go along with—readings, signing books, and TV appearances. Reviews in the printed press had been scarce. What I wrote did not often meet with the approval of over-sophisticated critics, who were overfed with the abundance of the literary market and always on the lookout for the "unusual" and "new approaches". Thomas had repeatedly told me I could make much more money—for me and for him—if I would take a more active part in the promotion of my books and give up my pen name, using my real one. Now I was ready to give him his chance. It was a chance for me too, because when I was going to commute between Ireland and Switzerland, a bit more money wouldn't hurt.

Anna met me at the airport with the car. She took in my new appearance with incredulous eyes.

"You've become a beauty," she said, "your face was always lovely, but now it's beautiful because you look so happy."

We hugged. Back home I showed her the scars on my body, which didn't look exactly pretty.

"Ts ts ts," she said, "I can do something about some of them, but a little plastic surgery wouldn't hurt."

"No! Niall and I agree about our scars. We'll live with them and won't hide them any more. They're part of our bond. They've become precious to us. They're proof of the miracles that can happen against all odds and reason."

Anna understood.

There remained the visit to Thomas's office. His eyes went big and round when he saw me.

"I never! With those looks you're going to be our promotional flagship!"

"Oh dear, that sounds scary!"

"You'll do great, don't worry. The PRs will draw up a campaign and do nothing you won't approve. Now tell me, who was the surgeon who did that fantastic job on you? I might pay him a visit myself."

I was prepared for this question. "He doesn't want his name disclosed, and I don't either. It was a very risky operation, and he won't ever do it again on anyone. It gave him the creeps, and he isn't going to advertise his achievement."

This was the exact truth, and it was all Thomas would ever know. He was pleased with the new manuscript, finding it quite atypical compared to my other texts.

"Well, well, well! Much more spirit here and less lukewarm romance, if I may say so. That should go well with the PR campaign—the author finally coming out of her shell and venturing onto new literary paths." He had no idea how right he was about the shell.

We agreed the new book would be ready in about three months in time for the annual Basel Book Fair in November. This time I would get a hardcover and a starting edition of 10,000. When I took my leave, Thomas made a clumsy attempt at chivalry, brushing the knuckles of my hand with a kiss.

The next thing I wanted to do was talk to Mark. He happened to be on a teaching assignment in Germany. We talked on the phone. I could feel how happy he was for me.

"I owe all this to you," I said. "Without you I would never have gone to Ireland, never have got rid of the shell, and never have met Niall."

"You owe it to yourself that you were up to the challenge," said Mark.

We agreed that he would come to visit us in Ireland as soon as possible.

***

After taking care of all the stuff you have to do when you want to move your life to another country, I was on a flight to Dublin again. Niall met me at the airport. We drove to Kinvara and I hardly recognized the cottage when we arrived. He had it freshly whitewashed, had added a conservatory to the front overlooking the Bay of Galway, and had done painting on the inside. The fireplace was fully functional again; a few blocks of peat were waiting to be lit.

At night he led me to the master bedroom. I shook with nervousness.

"Don't be afraid, little turtle," he whispered into my ear. "Let me take care of you. I'll be gentle."

He was.

From then on I knew I could trust him not only with my soul, but with my body too. Soon I could match his passion in every way, never getting enough of his touch.

Lux took his leave. Not for good, he signalled; he would still be here if needed.

Niall and I came to a point in our emotional and spiritual journey we hadn't thought possible. There were small rebounds from time to time, when difficult memories from the past and old insecurities got either to him or to me, or sometimes to both of us, but we always found a way to work things out. Very rarely did we have to call Lux; usually his appearance alone helped to sort things out.

In the eighth month of our life together I noticed changes in my body, and I could tell Niall we were going to have a child. We hadn't really thought about becoming parents but had just let our passion take its course. I suppose we were asking for what happened, and we were not unhappy about it at all.

With the pregnancy progressing, another wish of mine became true. My breasts started filling out. Sometimes Niall pulled me onto his lap and let his head rest on the new round softness, enjoying it as much as I did.

Then and there in one of those magic moments we promised each other to do everything in our power that our child, and the possible children that might follow, would never have to repeat their parents' ordeal, would never have to hide their minds and bodies behind hard shells.

The End

About the Author

After a long career as a journalist and translator, Esther Murbach decided to do what she had always wanted, to become a novelist. Since 2009 she has published three books in German. *The Turtle Woman* is her first book written in English. The mother of two adult daughters lives in Basel, Switzerland.

About the Book

Emily is a Swiss woman with a unique disfigurement: a shell covers her body. Successful as a writer but privately resigned to a life without love, she undertakes a trip to Ireland to explore her partly Irish roots. This proves to be a turning point in her life. She discovers a spiritual bond with the Emerald Isle and meets a man who is her counterpart. Niall, an Irish patriot, guesses what her condition is and where it comes from, because he had once experienced it himself. He offers her his understanding and help. They open up to each other, disclosing their dark secrets. In a difficult and painful process Emily overcomes her physical and emotional boundaries with Niall's assistance. Together they start on an emotional and spiritual journey as soul mates. Niall takes Emily to the Aran Island of Inishmore, where she meets her Irish grandmother for the first time. A few obstacles have to be overcome before Emily and Niall finally understand where their happiness lies.